I0585900

# MUSE

SAVING ABBIE BOOK 4

MAGGIE ALABASTER

Lock Me In
Written by Beau Pennington

Locked by reality,
Caught up in the flow.
Shaken by the maelstrom,
Ripped to the bone.

Shattered like glass,
Scattered dust and ash.
Pounded by the driving rain,
Torn by lightning flash.

Touched by hands that torment,
Held by arms that bind.
Soothed by words that have no meaning,
Mistaken by the past.

Take me by the heart,
Make me real again.
Heal my soul with something true,
Or let me cling to my imagination.

Give me something new.
Don't hold my scars against me,

Or mistakes I've made.
Lock me with reality, before I start to fade.
Lock me with reality, before I start to fade.

ABBIE

"I ASKED YOU A QUESTION." I turned around slowly. "What are you doing here, Pete?"

My former lover, owner of my old label, wore trousers and a button down shirt. They were looser than when I saw him last. His hair, once an inky black, was now grey at the temples. Fine lines surrounded eyes of faded blue. His skin was a shade or two darker than a tan. A day or two of scruff coated his chin.

Pietro Rossi was an attractive man. Even now, I saw why I fell for his charms.

At the same time, I wanted to deck the guy.

He gave me a lopsided smile that was too charming for anyone's own good. "Would you believe I got lost on the way to the men's room?"

"Considering the clear signage, no." I crossed my arms over my chest. "Try again. Or better yet, fuck off."

I made to push past him and head for the door.

He grabbed my arm. "I saw you come in here and followed you," he said quickly. "You know me, I'm impulsive."

I snorted a bitter laugh. "I remember."

One minute he was comforting me after I found out the man I thought I loved, Vance, only married me to further his own career. The next minute, Pete was kissing me and we were tearing off each other's clothes.

Yeah, okay, he wasn't the only impulsive one. I was just the one who got screwed over when Pete got back together with his wife and she insisted I be kicked off the label.

It didn't seem to have taken much persuasion on her part.

"Calista is dead," he said softly. "She...went for a swim and was taken by a shark."

He looked sad, confused, if not quite grieving. Their marriage was not what I would call rock solid, but that was a shocking, if incredibly rare way for someone to die.

I felt slightly bad for him for thinking that was

how she died. Of course, I couldn't tell him she was very much *not* taken by a shark.

I saw her disembodied head in a box in Adelaide. Jackson, the manager of Wolf Venom, the band my guys were a part of, sent her head back to Melbourne to be dealt with by Asher's sister, Rose.

Evidently, Rose had dealt with it. I didn't know if I approved of her method, but it wouldn't cast suspicion on me or any of my guys. I had to give her credit for creativity.

It also wouldn't cast any suspicion on Pete, which I thought was the plan. Asher wanted to pin her death, and that of Vance, on Pete as retribution for screwing me over.

Okay, it was extreme but that was Asher for you. He only wanted what was best for me and the rest of the guys.

"That's terrible," I said sincerely. "I'm so sorry. That still doesn't explain what you're doing in a women's toilet in Singapore airport. Did you follow me just to tell me that?" I shook off his arm and stepped away from him.

His eyes tracked me across the room. He reminded me of some kind of predator looking for its prey. He wouldn't find it here. At least, not with me. Not again.

"I sold the label," he said. "Calista insisted. She said I was more interested in work than her."

"I detect no lie here," I said dryly.

I met her plenty of times when she was alive. She was the kind of woman who saw everyone and everything as competition that she needed to step over on her way to getting what she wanted. It was my understanding she broke up with him because he was at work more than he was at home. Of course, the moment she found out he slept with me, she wanted him back. She would have only played second fiddle to the label for so long.

"Yeah." Pete stared down at the immaculately clean, tiled floor. "My work was my life and now…"

"Now you regret selling the label, because the reason for doing it is gone?"

Were we having a therapy session now? I didn't sign up for any of this. What the hell was new? A lot happened when I was with Onyx Riot Records that I didn't sign up for.

He shrugged. "I'm at a loose end. I thought I would travel, but I didn't expect to see you—"

"Bullshit," I snapped. "A quick search on your phone and you would know exactly where I would be and when. Not to mention your industry contacts. What is this really about? Your wife died and you thought you would track me down and see if I would spread my legs for you again?" I wanted to high five him in the face, with a chair.

He narrowed his eyes. "You make it sound so sleazy. So what if I wanted to see you again?" He took a couple of steps forward, forcing me to step back until the side of my hip was pressed against the sink.

"It is sleazy," I said in disgust. "She's barely cold and you're chasing after me."

"This isn't about her," he said evenly. "Before I sold the label, I was talking to a divorce lawyer. I was done with her. I shouldn't have taken her back after she found out about us. I fucked up. What I did to you was shitty."

"You think?" I said sarcastically. That was one word for it. I had many others, and tons for him. It started with 'asshole' and went all the way down to...

Okay, I don't know any obscenities that start with Z, but if there was one, he was it.

"I'll understand if you never forgive me. All I want is the chance to prove I can be a better man. The kind a woman like you deserves." He gave me his best puppy dog eyes I knew all too fucking well.

"For the longest time I thought you were exactly the kind of guy I deserved," I said. "You and Vance. I figured I must be a crappy person to have people do crappy things to me like you two did."

He stroked the back of his hand down my cheek. "Abbie, you are not a crappy person."

I jerked my face away from him. "Oh, I know that now. I have more love and support than I know what to do with. I have guys who would do anything for me."

"Guys?" he repeated. He looked confused. "Plural? What the—"

"Abbie?" Asher's voice echoed through the bathroom. "Are you okay in there?"

"I'm fine," I said without taking my eyes off Pete. "I was just about to come out."

"We're coming in there if you don't." That was Zeke's voice.

"We might anyway," Tully said. "Did I hear a man in there?"

"It's no one," I said firmly. No one important to me anymore. Seeing him was actually therapeutic. Now I knew I put that part of my life behind me, once and for all. I could move on and stop looking back so much.

"It doesn't look like no one," Tully said as he stepped through the doorway. He was followed by Zeke and Asher, and then the other three members of Wolf Venom. Even Penn. All six of them were big, muscular, tattooed rock gods.

And none of them looked impressed to see Pete.

"He looks familiar." Asher cocked his head at Pete. "Have we met?" He stepped closer and held out his hand to Pete. "I'm Asher, one of Abbie's boyfriends."

Pete mouthed, "One of..." He didn't take Asher's hand. "I know who you are. Abbie is touring with you. You don't have to pretend—"

Asher dropped his hand to his side and shrugged. His ego was healthy enough the snub wouldn't make a dent.

"We're not pretending." Zeke moved to my side and placed an arm around my shoulders. "I know who you are and I know what you did to Abbie. You thought it was okay to destroy her career because you couldn't keep your cock in your pants. Fortunately, she had enough talent to overcome your crap."

"She's talented enough." Pete shrugged. "I'm sure it helps if she's fucking all of you. She was always energetic. And happy to put it out." Of course he would fall back on cheap insults when he was backed into a corner. That was typical Pete right there.

"You're not as smart as you look, are you?" Landon asked. The blue-haired bassist crossed his arms over his chest. "Because if you are, you would realise you're outnumbered." He raised one eyebrow, just slightly. He was adorable and threatening at the same time.

"Would six against one be fair though?" Channing asked.

Landon looked at him sideways. "I suppose not, but one of us could punch the shit out of him without breaking a sweat."

"Those would be fairer odds," Channing agreed. He seemed satisfied with that.

"Asshole looks like he's about to piss his pants," Penn remarked. "For the record, she's not fucking all of us."

"Yet," Tully said.

Penn didn't deny that but he didn't agree with it either. He just stepped out of the way when a woman entered the bathroom and gave them all a funny look.

"We should get out of here," Zeke said. "We wouldn't want to distract anyone from what they need to do." He jerked his head towards the door.

Judging by the way the woman was staring at them all with huge eyes, that was exactly what was happening already. It wasn't every day a person saw six gorgeous rock stars in the women's toilets.

Probably.

"Yes," I agreed. "Let's get out of here. I've said everything I need to say." I eyed Pete, daring him to try to add anything else. I cared about him once, but now it was like looking at a stranger. One who made his own bed. Now he could sleep in it.

Alone. Or at least, not with me in it.

In spite of the guys, Pete couldn't help himself. "Abbie," he started tentatively, "I'm sorry for the shit I did. I'm sorry you got caught up in it. I really do care about you. When these guys get tired of you, or you get tired of them, look me up. I know you remember how good we were together. I made mistakes, but I could make it up to you if you let me try."

I doubted that very much. "If they get tired of me—"

"We won't," Asher said.

"Nope, never," Zeke agreed.

"That's a matter of opinion," Penn muttered.

I rolled my eyes at the keyboardist and started again. "If they get tired of me, I still wouldn't go back to you. I can do so much better. Hell, I would do a lot better being on my own than being with you."

If I wanted to be with someone who only spent time with me at their convenience, I would get a cat.

"You say that now," Pete started.

"She's made herself clear," Tully said. Somehow, he managed to be pleasant and threatening at the same time. Was that something he learnt during his training as an assassin, or was that it just him? Maybe a little of both. You probably couldn't learn how to kill people without learning how to intimidate them as well.

"Come on, let's go." Asher took my hand and led me toward the door. "There's this restaurant I want to take you to. It'll blow your mind."

"Me too?" Zeke asked. As if he would be left behind.

"All of us," Asher said.

I stepped out of the bathroom surrounded by my six guys and didn't look back.

## 2

------

ABBIE

"CAN YOU BELIEVE THAT GUY?" I said over a delicious bowl of rice.

"What guy?" Landon asked, an innocent expression on his face. "I don't remember a guy. Does anyone else remember a guy?"

"Not me," Channing agreed. He shoved the last of his apam balik into his mouth and started to chew around the huge mouthful.

I snorted a laugh, appreciative at their attempts to lighten the mood. "I don't want to remember the guy." My voice low, I told them what he said about Calista dying, and selling the label.

"Rose was always the creative one in the family," Asher mused. "Well, her and me. I would definitely have voted her most likely to come up with interesting ways to dispose of dead bodies."

Tully chewed thoughtfully on his roti. "He didn't say who he sold the label to, did he?"

I shook my head. "We didn't get that far. Why? Wait, don't tell me he sold it to Reuben Brantley?" I eyed Zeke. He was no fan of his mobster brother, or the rest of his family. Out of seven brothers, he was the only one not involved in the family business. Not for lack of trying on Reuben's part.

"No," Tully said. "He sold it to Xavier Lang. And he gave it to me."

I almost choked on my rice. Asher patted my back while Zeke handed me a glass of water.

When I finally got my breath back, I said, "I must be hearing things. Did you say you're the new owner of Onyx Riot Records?"

Tully shrugged. "Apparently so. That's what he said, but he was trying to distract me while his hired thugs took out Zeke."

"They weren't very good hired thugs," Zeke said.

"Judging by the fact you're still alive, I would say that's accurate," Asher said. "Thank fuck." He leaned over in his chair to give Zeke a side hug.

"What are you going to do with it?" Penn asked.

"A record label, I mean. We're not looking for a new one, are we?" He glanced around the table.

"No, we're not," Zeke said firmly. "That's a good question though. What the fuck are you gonna do with a record label?"

"No idea," Tully said. "I guess I'll hire someone to run it for me and let it make me money. While changing the culture of bullying that went on there." He inclined his head towards me.

"There's certainly room for improvement," I agreed. "Lots of it. I'm happy to tell you who works there and doesn't suck. They'll be more receptive than some of the others."

"Sounds like you need to put together a list of people to get rid of," Asher said.

"And by get rid of, you mean fire?" I raised an eyebrow at him.

"Fire, if you insist." Asher pretended to look sulky.

I was sure he would take out a hit on anyone I asked him to, but, like Zeke, he left the violence to his family. For the most part at least. He hadn't flinched when he put a gun to the head of the man who tried to attack us in Perth. Nor had he flinched when he pulled the trigger, killing the man and sending blood and brains flying.

Just thinking about it made my stomach turn and my panties wet. I'd started to accept that I was fucked up in the head for being turned on by shit like that.

I punched him lightly on the chest. "There's no need for anything worse than people losing their job. Even then, I prefer to give people a chance. The worst of them are gone now anyway, for the most part."

"That's something we can work on, but after the tour," Tully said. "It might be fun to run it when I retire from playing. In the meantime, I'll have to find out if Xavier was telling the truth or not. There's no point making plans for the label if I don't own it at all."

"What are you going to tell your mother?" Penn picked at a piece of chicken with his fork.

Tully sighed. "Not the truth. At some point, she's going to call me to tell me he's dead. I'll tell her we had drinks, then went our separate ways. If she knew why he was in Perth, she'll figure out what really happened, but she won't point the finger at me. She would never be able to prove I killed him anyway. No one would."

He hadn't lost the haunted look he'd had on his face when he turned up at Perth airport. For a trained assassin, he hated killing. Especially his adopted father. That was understandable.

"Giving you the label should work in your favour," Zeke reasoned. "What excuse would you have for killing him when he gave you such a generous gift?"

"That's a good point," Asher said. "Plus, with all the attacker's bodies lying around, it'll look like one of them did it."

"And if it didn't before, then it will after my brothers have finished with the scene," Zeke added.

For guys who kidnapped me twice and threatened me with rape, the twins made themselves useful in cleaning up after us. Of course, that was only because the people who attacked us, hired by Dante Fiorelli, went after them as well. It was a strange alliance and was unlikely to last, but if it helped us to get out of that shit, then we would put up with them for now.

"I still can't believe you can say things like that and keep a straight face," I said.

Zeke grinned. "It's a knack we've all developed over the years. When you talk about this shit enough it stops feeling like a big deal. You're getting pretty good at it yourself."

"Shit." I frowned. "Am I really?" Was I already that

desensitised to criminal activity and killing? I must be, because otherwise I would be having nightmares about Asher shooting a guy, and I'd be scared of the drummer.

Wouldn't I?

I couldn't imagine being scared of Asher. Underneath the big, muscular rock star exterior, he was a sweet and thoughtful guy. He would take out hits on people if I asked him to. No one said my guys and my relationship with them wasn't complicated.

Asher and Tully, on either side of me, leaned in and put their arms around me.

"You just roll with it," Asher said.

"You haven't had any other choice," Tully added. "You didn't ask to get involved with any of our shit, but that's what happened when you got involved with us. You could have walked away, but you didn't."

"Yet," Penn said.

"In spite of Penn being an asshole, you stuck around." Asher flashed a smile at the keyboardist.

Penn rolled his eyes in response and stabbed his fork into his chicken like it was Asher's eyeball. "Maybe she stuck around because I'm an asshole. She might have a type."

When everyone turned to stare at him, he looked

up. "What? We all saw that Pete guy. We know what Vance was like. The rest of you all have your asshole moments. Sounds like a type to me."

"Are you hoping it is?" Landon looked at him curiously.

Penn just tore into his chicken and shoved some of it into his mouth.

"I think that's a yes," Channing said.

I pushed my empty plate aside and rested my elbows on the table. I gripped my wine glass in both hands and looked into the reddish-purple liquid.

"I'd like to think if I have a type it's not assholes," I said. "I don't think any of you are assholes. Not even Penn, although you have your moments."

Naturally, I said that when his mouth was full so he couldn't retort.

He might have rolled his eyes toward the ceiling though. His exterior was a tougher façade than Asher or even Zeke but it was just that—a façade. Once or twice, I saw past it. Deep down, there was a decent guy in there. I was determined to find him. If I couldn't, then we would have to learn to put up with each other.

Landon rubbed his chin. "I think if you have a type it's musical, badass, tattooed—"

"With lots of muscles," Channing finished for him.

"Who wants to fuck you, not fuck you over," Zeke said.

"And love you," Asher said.

"And keep you safe," Tully said.

All eyes turned to Penn. He washed down his chicken with a gulp of beer. "Who may or may not be assholes once in a while."

I found myself wiping a tear off my cheek. I waved Asher away when he looked concerned. "It's not a sad tear. It's happy tears. If that's my type, it sounds pretty fucking perfect to me. It sums up all of you. As long as the asshole part is only once in a while."

Who wouldn't want a group of guys like that? One of these days I was going to wake up and find all of this was a dream. A very long, very detailed, very hot dream, but still. How could any of this be real?

"I make no promises." Penn toasted me with his beer glass, then drank the rest down in a gulp.

We drank and finished eating in silence after that before I broke it with the question we were probably all thinking.

"So, do you think this—Fiorelli—will try to come after us again here in Singapore, or somewhere else in the world?"

I turned my gaze to Zeke, who was the official lead singer and unofficial leader of the band. And usually the one who had the answers to these kinds of questions.

"It's possible," he admitted, "but if they were trying to extend their influence across Australia, then probably not. They'll turn their attention to the rest of my family first. Either they'll try to kill Reuben or Reuben will try to kill them. Or they'll go after the Bells and vice versa. This shit gets ugly, if you haven't noticed."

I had. I really had.

"Any idea who might come out on top?" I asked.

"Ideas? A few. Answers? Not really. If someone does, it won't last. There's always somebody ready to step in and stir up shit. It's like that game where you hammer down one animal that pops up and another one pops up." He traced circles with the condensation on the table.

"Whack-a-mole?" Channing suggested.

Zeke pointed a finger gun at him. "Yeah, that. We weren't big on games like that as kids. We usually played hide and seek and ran around pretending to shoot each other with sticks."

"Why am I not surprised?" I couldn't quite imagine him as a little boy, but it was more plausible than his older brothers. Of the ones I'd met, they both seemed like they could use some childish fun once in a while. Maybe they wouldn't be such dick-heads if they enjoyed themselves more.

Zeke grinned. "Because you've met four of my brothers. Believe me, Joshua and Lucas aren't any better. I don't think Joshua has ever smiled in his life. And Lucas, he's more like Reuben than the rest of us. He's ruthless when it comes to getting what he wants. He also has the same charm as the twins, which means never turn your back on him and don't trust what he says. Everything to him is a game with some kind of end goal."

"Lucky you have us as brothers now," Asher said. "And we have you."

"And we all have each other," Tully said. He looked thoughtful. It didn't take a genius or a mind reader to know what he was thinking.

I leaned into him. "I know you're not okay, but if there's anything I can do..." I didn't even know what to say in the circumstances. 'Hey, I know you killed your father because he was about to kill you, but you'll be fine.'

Yeah, even in my head it didn't sound right.

"Just keep being you," he said. "That's all I ask."

I smiled. "I can do that. I don't know how to be anyone else anyway."

"Me either," he whispered.

# 3

## PENN

"Good evening, Singapore!" Zeke shouted into the microphone. "There's something I wanna know." He lowered the microphone to give them a moment to absorb what he said and cheer.

The guy could be a tosser at times, but he knew how to get the audience going.

Not that they needed it most of the time. I mean, we were Wolf fucking Venom. People were hyped up long before we got on stage.

Long before the support act, Blazing Violet, performed.

Before Abbie performed the few songs Levi Jones decided to shoehorn between the support act and us.

Yeah, okay, she wasn't *too* bad and she usually didn't kill the vibe Blazing Violet started, but when we were first told she was joining us on tour, I was as pissed as fuck. I expected her to be nothing more than an airhead distraction with her pretty face and gorgeous, fuckable body. We didn't need her along for the ride. We were fine as we were.

Sure my eyes followed her ass when she walked across the stage. Okay, so she was the one I thought about when I slid my hand up and down my cock. Women like her were still dangerous. They had a way of getting under your skin.

Just like she got under mine.

Because they suck, my asshole bandmates saw it long before I did. Long before I wanted to admit it to myself.

What good would come from admitting it anyway? She was fucking Zeke, Asher and Tully. It was only a matter of time before she fell into bed with Channing and Landon. That was the definition of handful and pussy full.

Where would I even fit into that picture?

The worst thing? It was more than lust. For weeks I've stood back, watching them fall for her, and her for them. They were all becoming dangerously intertwined, like a sticky spiderweb. And none of them could have been happier.

I shook my head and turned my attention back to

Zeke.

He raised his microphone back to his lips. "I want to know if you can be louder than the audiences in Australia."

Fifty-five thousand people in National Stadium cheered, clapped and stamped their feet.

Zeke smiled. "Is that the best you can do? Come on, I want them to hear you back in Australia!"

The audience responded louder this time, just like every other concert ever. It never seemed to get old with crowds. Honestly, I wasn't sure it really mattered what Zeke said. It was his presence they wanted. To see the real Zeke Brantley, lead singer of one of the biggest bands in the world, standing on stage in front of their eyes. And their phones. He could have told them they were all goldfish with bowler hats and smelly armpits and they would have cheered.

I made a mental note to dare him to do that sometime.

"That's better." Zeke grinned. "I bet they can hear you in Sydney."

I snorted. If that was the case, we would all be deaf right now. Of course, he had to say shit like that. The audience ate it all up, even though everyone knew it was crap.

Zeke nodded and we launched into our first song of the night.

This was what I lived for. Literally sometimes. Being up on stage, playing for a huge crowd. People who were willing to part with a shit load of money to hear our music. We played covers here and there, when a song was good enough, but it's one thing to regurgitate someone else's creativity and another thing to put your own on display.

There was no bigger rush in the entire fucking universe then hearing a stadium full of people sing your lyrics back to you. They listened to songs I wrote on repeat. Over and over until they learned every word, because they wanted to. Because listening to it gave them pleasure. It was like fingering fifty thousand people at once, and knowing every single one of them would come.

Multiple times.

Nothing got me going more than this. A tiny voice in the back of my mind reminded me that Abbie got me going as much as this, but I ignored it. What did the little voice in the back of my head know about anything anyway? That same little voice would be happy if I let myself get lost in her like the rest of the guys.

Stupid prick.

My fingers caressed my keyboard. I let myself get lost in a much safer space. Notes, chords and tempo, the swell of the audience, the other instruments complementing mine. For about ten seconds, I was able to forget about Abbie.

Then the song ended and she came back on stage. *Fuuuck.*

She was gorgeous in a short black dress that fit her in all the right places. Her ass looked like absolute perfection. The front showed just the right amount of cleavage.

I pictured myself tugging it down to expose her nipples. I imagined her looking down at me as I first sucked one, and then the other. I would roll the dress down her hips and off her long, shapely legs.

In my imagination, she wore a black lace G-string that was basically see-through at the front. Like the pair she wore in the hotel in Perth when I watched Tully fuck her while the other guys fucked each other.

And... if I kept thinking this way, fifty-five thousand people were going to see me get very hard. See, she's dangerous.

I grabbed my water bottle and took a few quick gulps. It wasn't a cold shower, but it would do for now.

I caught Asher's eye and the motherfucker grinned at me like he knew exactly what I was thinking. Hell, he could probably see from where he sat behind his drums. Dickhead.

I flicked the open end of the water bottle in his direction, but he only smiled wider as cold water hit his chest and face and trickled down his skin.

"Thanks, that was refreshing," he shouted.

I closed the bottle and put it back as Zeke and Abbie took centre stage, microphones in their hands.

On the signal from Zeke, I started to play the music to back up their singing. I didn't know why I bothered. I doubted anyone in the audience was aware I was playing at all. When those two sang together, no one seemed to notice anything but them. No one could deny they had chemistry. The way they had their hands all over each other while they performed, they might as will be fucking out there.

The crowd loved it.

I slipped back into my own little world until their second song was finished.

Then it was my time to shine. I mean, more than I already was.

The rest of the band left the stage, leaving me to my keyboard and the audience.

It was one song, but the chance to play by myself to that many people was huge for me. I didn't have as big an ego as the rest of the guys in the band.

Yeah, really. People would fucking laugh if I told them that, but that doesn't make it not true.

Ever since I first put my fingers on piano keys, playing was my entire life. I had a talent for it. A gift. At the same time, it was a curse. For years, I wanted to be seen past the piano. I wanted to be Beau Pennington, a kid. When I realised people were never going to look past my musical ability, I learned to embrace it.

Being alone out here was part of that.

I leaned toward the microphone. "Hey. How is your evening going?"

The roar of the crowd was like a tsunami of sound, washing over me, carrying me away to some other place. A place where only me and them existed. The rest of the world was gone, filtered out with a roar of appreciation.

Yeah, that's fucking poetic isn't it? That was how I felt. Sue me.

"I thought I'd play a little song for you. You might know it." I told the guys I didn't know what song I was going to play until I played it, and I didn't for the most part. Tonight, though, I wanted to play something I wrote. Something that spoke of the guy I kept deep down in the darkest parts of me. The guy I both wanted Abbie to touch, and was terrified she'd learn existed. The guys knew about him but not how deep he went, or how dark he really was.

I put my fingers on the keys and started to play "Lock Me In".

I didn't have quite the calibre of vocal talent Zeke did, but what I lacked in ability, I made up for in feeling the lyrics and putting all of my emotion into them. There were a lot of those. This song was about the darkest time in my life. A time when I had no idea if there would be a tomorrow, or if I even wanted there to be one.

If it wasn't for the guys, there wouldn't be.

In the corner of my eye, I saw fifty-five thousand phones with their lights on, waving back and forth in the air.

That was it. No one shouted, cheered or clapped. The audience got lost in the song the same way I did. For those three and a half minutes, the whole stadium shared the same perfect moment.

I let the notes die away and slumped forward a little. A second or two of silence was followed by rousing applause and shouts for more.

There wouldn't be more, not tonight. This was

my moment, but it was enough. If I wanted to, I could go off by myself, solo, but this one song was plenty to satisfy my ego. The rest of the night, I would happily hide amongst the guys out here on stage.

"That was awesome." Zeke slapped me on the back on the way past.

"Yeah, never better." Tully slipped the strap of his guitar back over his head.

"You should do your own songs more often." Asher slipped behind his drums and picked his sticks back up.

"Maybe," I said noncommittally. I glanced towards the hydraulic stairs that lead backstage, but they were already closed. I couldn't even admit to myself I was hoping for a glimpse of Abbie.

I liked their approval, thrived on it, but that little voice in the back of my head wanted hers as well.

Hell, if I was her, I would flip me off, not give me praise. I hadn't been subtle in my annoyance at her joining the tour. And I was happy to tell her when I found her irritating. Only, that happened less and less often those days.

Not that I would let her know that, no way. The sooner she realised I really was an asshole, the better off we would all be.

No one ever said I wasn't as conflicted as fuck. In fact, they would probably tell you that was my default mode, conflicted and snarky, with a side of sarcastic asshole.

"You fucking killed it." Landon picked up his bass guitar, the bright purple and black one, and grinned at me.

I shrugged one shoulder. "It was okay." It was more than okay. It felt really fucking good. Better than sex. That was another good reason to stay away from Abbie. If sex with her was better than this, I'd be spoilt for life.

At least, that was what I told myself. I told myself a lot of things. Some of them made more sense than others.

"You're a rock god and you know it," Channing said. He picked up his saxophone and placed his hands on the keys, ready for the next song.

"Get it on a bumper sticker," I said. "Or a T-shirt."

Channing laughed and put his mouthpiece to his lips. More of the guys should play woodwind instruments. It was a good way of shutting them up.

I shifted on my stool to make myself comfortable and waited for the signal from Zeke.

# 4

ABBIE

"I've been speaking to Levi," Jackson said slowly.

His tone was ominous, or maybe I was paranoid. He pinned us down at breakfast while we all sat in the hotel restaurant eating bacon, eggs and toast, and drinking too much coffee.

If too much coffee is actually possible. Is it? Let's go with no.

"About?" Zeke prompted. He gave the band's manager the side eye. His fork was poised over his eggs as if he might use it on Jackson instead.

Jackson cleared his throat. Yep, that was definitely ominous. "I was thinking it's time we took Penn's performance to the next level."

Penn scowled. "It doesn't need... wait a minute, am I getting that motherfucking grand piano I've been asking for for years?" He pumped the air with his fist. The expression on his face was the closest thing to a smile I ever saw on him. He actually looked excited.

Jackson appeared to be less enthusiastic. "Not exactly, no."

"A baby grand is fine," Penn ventured. "Or an upright." He was grasping at straws and from the expression on his face he knew it. "Raised platform?"

Jackson shook his head. "I was thinking, and Levi agrees, that you could sing with Abbie."

What the fuck?

Penn stared. First at Jackson, then at me. He had FUCK LIFE tattooed across his knuckles. Right now, he had his L finger pointed at my chest. "Did you put him up to this?"

I frowned at him. "What? This is the first I've heard of it too."

Penn dropped his hand to the table with a thud. Cups and plates rattled, and coffee nearly sloshed onto the table. "It's not fucking happening. That's my solo. You can screw with whatever the hell else you want, but not that."

He'd gone from ecstatic to furious so quickly I almost got whiplash.

At the same time, I understood why he was

pissed off. Jackson hadn't even asked either of us. To spring something like this on Penn and me, in front of the whole band, seemed unfair.

"It would be awesome," Asher said tentatively. "You two would sound—"

"No." Penn slammed his fist down on the table so hard we all jumped. "We fucking wouldn't." He shoved back his chair so hard it screeched on the floor, then stalked away out the door.

"That went well," Channing said ironically.

Tully's eyes followed Penn until he was out of sight. "I should go after him. He might do something stupid."

"Give him some time," Zeke said. "He'll calm down. One of us can talk to him when he has his head on straight." He looked over to Jackson. "You didn't think he would be happy about that, did you?"

Jackson shrugged. "I figured he'd go off initially, but when he calms down, he'll realise I'm right. The audiences will love it."

"Does Abbie want to do it?" Asher gave me a questioning look. Apparently he was the only one who remembered I might have an opinion on the subject.

Did I?

"Not if it's going to create friction, no," I said.

When it came to Penn, I hadn't done anything *but* create friction since I joined the tour. Most of it wasn't even the good kind of friction.

"Penn will be fine," Jackson said. "It doesn't even need to be an every night thing. You won't be on tour with the guys forever. While we are, we might as well make good use of you and lift your profile as much as we can."

"Right." Of course, it wasn't just about me or Penn. Like every aspect of this industry, it was a business decision. Whatever it took to make the label more money in the long run was what mattered. Including ensuring artists had career longevity.

I wouldn't complain if I had that, but I didn't want to feel like I was stepping on Penn to get there. He certainly didn't need me to lift his profile. Unless he planned to go solo someday. In which case, this was a good move. Jackson and Levi might know things I didn't.

I mean, of course they did, it was their job to know.

"When he calms down, you can talk about what song you're going to sing and get in some rehearsal." Jackson looked like the matter was settled and we would have to deal with that whether we liked it or not.

I suspected he hoped it would be that simple, but I doubted Penn would come around that easily.

"I'll see you all later." Jackson gulped down the last of his coffee and slipped out of the restaurant.

"Well that was... different," Landon said. "You have to love it when your manager drops a bomb right in the middle of breakfast."

"It keeps life interesting," Asher said.

Zeke snorted. "That's one word for it, babe."

Tully was still watching the door, a worried expression on his face.

I chose my words carefully. "When you say Penn might do something stupid..."

Tully turned to me and the left side of his mouth drew back. "You know about his past?"

"Only what the tabloids mentioned," I said. "I also know how much they like to make things up." Most of those kinds of magazines should be in the fiction section.

Or better yet, not exist at all.

Zeke leaned forward and rested his elbows on the table. "Some of it is accurate. He did actually overdose." He looked down at his coffee cup and continued with glazed eyes, his voice a whisper.

"That was during the early days of the band. We were the ones who found him. I thought he was dead when I first walked into the hotel room."

The memory clearly rattled him, even now.

I put a hand on Zeke's arm and squeezed his rock hard bicep. "That must have been terrible." Even if you got used to death, it would be different when it was a friend. And to find him like that... They all must have been devastated.

"It was pretty shit," Zeke agreed. "We were lucky we got him to hospital in time. Another hour or two and he would have been gone."

"And all his talent with him," Tully added.

"What a fucking waste," Asher said softly.

Zeke nodded slowly. "It would have been. It's not the first time he OD'd either. The first time, he was seventeen. He was full of rage because his parents planned his life out for him." The sides of his mouth tugged back.

"They gave him options," Asher said ironically.

Zeke laughed bitterly. "Yeah, concert pianist or lawyer. Nothing else would live up to their standards. They pushed him so hard, I'm surprised he didn't give up the piano entirely. Walk away to get them off his back."

"He loves it too much for that," Tully said.

"Lucky for us." Zeke curled his hands around his coffee cup. "And him. Anyway, he claims the first time was an accident, but I wonder if it really was. "

"You think he tried to take his own life?" I asked as gently as I could. I was starting to understand why Penn was the way he was. It couldn't be easy having parents who made life choices for you. Who pushed you so hard, even if it was in a direction you might want to go. Who made you think you had no options left.

"Possibly." Zeke took a sip of his coffee. He must have found it cold, because he grimaced. "He was a pretty messed up kid. But, you know, how would he have known what the right dose was? That sort of thing is easy to screw up."

I nodded and squeezed Zeke's arm. "And the second time? Also an accident?"

"As far as we know," Asher said. "It's the last time he touched the stuff."

"It better be the last time ever," Zeke growled. "We signed with White Wolf Records shortly after that. There's a clause in his contract that if he even touches drugs, he's out."

"Out as in?" I asked.

"Out of the band," Zeke said. "Out of his contract. Out of his career, unless another label will touch him. He agreed to it. I'm not sure if he was the one who suggested it in the first place, to make sure he had extra incentive to stay clean."

"Levi Jones smokes weed," I pointed out.

"Levi isn't addicted to it," Asher said. After a moment, he frowned. "Not that we know of anyway." He looked around the table but no one disagreed with him.

"Penn hates the smell of weed," Zeke said. "It's other shit he was into. Harder stuff than dope. For the record, he would be just as out if he smoked weed. These days it's just Ibuprofen and alcohol for the boy."

"I've noticed he doesn't drink very much," I remarked. "Not excessively anyway."

"I'll get plastered when I know I won't wake up in Sydney working for my brother," Zeke said. "Until then, we all keep it low key."

"Besides, hangovers suck," Asher said.

"Truth," Tully agreed.

I turned to the lead guitarist. "So when Penn stormed out like that, you're worried he might find some drugs and…use them?"

"It crossed my mind." Tully started to stack the empty plates in a neat pile for the server to collect.

"He's more likely to do something stupid when he's angry."

"That solo means a lot to him though," Landon said. "He wouldn't risk that. At least, I don't think he would." His brow wrinkled adorably.

"He better not," Zeke growled. "Otherwise Abbie can take his spot and he can float around as a pissed off ghost." He smirked in the direction of the door.

"Just what I need." I grimaced. "To spend the rest of my life haunted by the ghost of Penn. I'd wake up in the middle of the night to the sound of piano music."

"At least he doesn't play the tuba." Channing grinned. "Not professionally, I mean."

"I couldn't replace him if he did," I said. "I can't play the tuba." I wouldn't want to replace him anyway. I could play the keyboard, but nowhere near as well as him. Nor did I know the band's songs well enough. Nor did I want anything bad to happen to Penn.

"It's never too late to learn," Asher said. "I've always wanted to play something like that. But then I remind myself I already play an instrument that's loud and potentially obnoxious." He grinned.

"That sums you up perfectly," Zeke teased. "Loud and potentially obnoxious."

Asher laughed. "I think obnoxious but potentially loud might be more accurate. That sums up all of us."

"Speak for yourself," Tully said dryly. "I'm not obnoxious."

"Says you," Landon said.

I sat back and listened to them talk about who was obnoxious and who wasn't. Insults and teasing flew this way and that, but their banter made me smile. They were so comfortable with each other, even after Penn stalked out.

I have to admit, after what they told me about him, I was worried too. I would have to find some time to talk to him and work things out. I didn't want him to throw away his life and career because of me, and I didn't want him angry at me anymore. I would have to make him realise this wasn't my idea. Never in a million years would it have occurred to me that Penn's solo was anything other than his moment.

Now the idea was out there, it was hard not to think about it. Singing with Penn would be interesting, to say the least.

## 5

ABBIE

"Hey, asshole." I crossed my arms and stood watching Penn play.

It didn't take a genius to realise where Penn stomped off to. I didn't know him as well as I knew some of the other guys, but when music was someone's happy place, it tended to be the place we turned to when we needed comfort.

It was a short walk to the stadium for our sound check for tonight's concert, our only one in Seoul, Korea. Shame, I loved Korean food and K-pop. Korean dramas too, when I had the time to watch them. It would have been fun to stay here for a while longer. I'd have to find time to come back when the tour was over and spend a week or two.

In the meantime, we had a sound check to do, but

I asked the rest of the guys to stay backstage while I spoke to Penn.

He didn't even look up. "Fuck off."

If we became friends and actually liked each other, we would probably still talk to each other the same way. The insults were strangely comfortable, like the guys' banter, or an old pair of shoes. The kind you should throw away but just can't bring yourself to do it.

"So eloquent." I didn't recognise the song he was playing, but when he stopped to scribble on a piece of paper beside him, I realised he was writing it. Usually, I would leave someone alone while they were in the midst of the creative process. In this case, he would have to suck it up. Things needed to be said.

"That's me," he said. "I'm all about being classy as shit."

I snorted, because I was also really classy. "A part of that is right."

He looked up at me and smirked. "Yeah, the classy bit." He leered unashamedly at the way my cleavage was pushed up by my arms.

"Keep telling yourself that." I lowered my arms to my sides.

"This might surprise you, but I don't need your

permission to do a fucking thing," he said coldly.

"No you don't," I agreed. "Except listen to me for one minute."

The motherfucking smartass raised his smart-watch to his lips and said, "Set a timer for sixty seconds." He lowered his arm and raised an eyebrow. "You're on the clock."

I rolled my eyes. Since he was probably being literal, I said, "You know I had nothing to do with Jackson's suggestion, right? I didn't go to him and say, 'Hey, you know how Penn drives me absolutely nuts? Well let's screw with his day by making his solo a duet instead.'"

"Because it didn't occur to you to do that?" Penn asked. "You would have sooner or later."

I barked a laugh. "If I wanted to mess up your day, I would think of something more creative. Like putting lemon juice in your water bottle, or filling your shoes with confetti. Now I'm thinking about it, I still might do both of those things. But I had nothing to do with this. It—"

The timer went off.

"Time's up. For what it's worth, I didn't think you would come up with the stupid fucking idea. It's exactly the kind of shit Jackson and Levi pull."

"Because they're smart businessmen." I didn't

realise what I walked into until Penn raised his eyebrows.

"Because they're *smart*," he said.

"Meaning I'm not." He knew exactly what to say to get under my skin and get a response from me. Being called a dumb blond was certainly one of those things, and he knew it.

"You said it, not me," he said easily.

He looked so smug, I was tempted to punch him in the face. Since I'd only hurt myself, I wondered if Tully would mind if I hit Penn with his guitar. He would understand if I explained the context. Hell, it wasn't as though Tully didn't have half a dozen more guitars he could use.

Lucky for Penn, I didn't want any musical instruments to be damaged in the process of this conversation. No guitar deserved that.

"You've really embraced the whole tortured rock star thing haven't you?" I asked. "Like you're the only person in the world who has ever been through stuff."

His eyes flashed with anger. "You haven't got a fucking clue."

"Don't I?" I challenged. "Why don't you enlighten me?" Did I really think he would open up to me? No, not really, but one of us had to open a channel of communication. It might as well be me.

His jaw moved a couple of times, then he shook his head. "I see what you're trying to do."

I crossed my arms again, not caring I was showing a bunch of cleavage. Let him leer. "Yeah? What's that?"

"You think I'm going to tell you my life story, so you can tell me I'm full of shit and everything that happened to you is so much worse." He slapped his pencil down on his piece of paper and got up from his stool.

"Absolutely," I said sarcastically. "Because everything with me is a competition. Every shit thing in my life is twice as bad as every shit thing in your life." I laughed bitterly. "Is it so hard to believe I just want to listen to what you have to say?"

The look he gave me said it was.

"Are you going to insist on this duet bullshit?" He stepped away from his keyboard.

"What are you going to do if I insist?" I asked. "Let me guess, you'll sit on your stool, cross your arms and refuse to play or sing. Will you pout too?"

He gave me a venomous look and stalked away towards the back stage.

I should have let him be, but I followed him

instead. "See what I mean?" I said to his back. "You can't even have a civil conversation without storming off like a spoilt child. This might be news to you, but you can't always get what you want."

He turned around so fast I took a step back.

"Can't I?"

I was hardly aware of him moving again, but he grabbed my wrists, pulled them up and pinned me to the corridor wall. He pressed the length of his body to mine and slammed his lips down onto my mouth.

I was so surprised I didn't even think to protest. By the time I regained my breath, I realised I didn't want to. I kissed him and held nothing back. All of the anger and frustration became a burning desire. I wanted to feel every part of him on every part of me.

As he kissed me, he rubbed his body up and down against me. His already hard cock grazed my hip through the layers of clothes.

I let out a soft, needy moan.

He let my hands go and slid his up the front of my shirt to cup my breasts. His palms rubbed my nipples until they quickly became stiff, aching peaks.

I wound my arms around his neck as he moved his mouth from mine, down to my throat.

"I still hate you," he murmured against my skin.

"Got it." I snaked one arm from his neck down his

chest, over his rock hard stomach to his equally rock hard cock. "I hate you too." Since we were more or less alone, but not caring if we were anyway, I undid the front of his jeans, releasing his erection into my eager fingers.

"Fuck." He seemed to be resisting the urge to pump himself into my hand. He slipped his hand down my side, over my ass, and pulled up my thigh until my knee was at his hip. He held it there while his hand ghosted across the front of my panties and delved into the gap at the side.

"Figures you're as wet as fuck already." He pressed two fingers into me and stroked my insides until I was panting. "Practically dripping."

I didn't know how he had words because I had fucking none right then. Even fewer when he pulled aside my panties and grabbed my wrists to pin them above my head again. He carefully placed his cock outside the entrance to my pussy and, with no restraint or hesitation, pressed all the way, balls-deep into me.

I bit my lip to keep from screaming out in pleasure. For a guy who could behave like a big cock, he also had a big cock. He certainly knew how to use it. He drove it into me hard, but at the same time angled perfectly.

He massaged my clit with his fingertips like he knew exactly what he was doing. Hell, he'd undoubtedly had a lot of experience doing it. Whatever, I wasn't going to complain.

I rolled my hips in time with his thrusts and watched his face. His expression was a mask of concentration and pleasure. There was nothing hotter than a guy mid-fuck. Especially when I was the one getting fucked.

I half closed my eyes as the pressure started to build. "Shit, yeah."

"I know you're close, but wait," he ordered.

I groaned. "I don't think I can." I didn't think I *wanted* to. He played my body like he played his keyboard. Did he think he could bring me to crescendo and then hold me there as long as he wanted?

Yes, of course he did. Like always, he wanted to be in control.

"You can because I say you can," he said with certainty. "For once in your life, shut the fuck up and do as you're told."

"Yes, sir." It was meant to be sarcastic, but it didn't come out that way. It sounded breathless and submissive.

His eyes snapped up to my face and for the first

time ever, he smiled at me. "I like the sound of that. Say it again."

I was even closer to coming, but I managed to scrape together enough breath to say, "Yes, sir."

He groaned, a deep, guttural, animalistic sound that pushed me so close to the edge I might as well have been standing on a cliff with my toes poking off.

I screwed my eyes shut with the effort of not coming. "I need to..." I begged.

"Me too," he grunted. "Okay, you can come."

However he did it, he timed our orgasms to perfection. We were in sync like an orchestra who had played together for years. Like a band who knew each other so well, their music blended together to create something incredible.

Our voices were matching moans of pleasure and ragged pants of effort. The storm that washed over me was better than any music. It started in my core and spread to every part of my body until my toes curled and my hair stood on end.

When the waters finally started to recede, they washed over me again. And again.

By the third time, I was completely out of breath and could have sworn I'd seen stars in another universe, in another time, for an eternity.

We slumped together, sweaty and sticky, but oh so fucking satisfied. We stayed like that for a couple of minutes before he slid out of me and pulled my panties back into place. He even put my skirt back down, although the front was crumpled.

I didn't care. We hadn't done anything to be ashamed of.

At least, that was what I thought until he said, "I can't get everything I want, can I? Seems to me, I can." He looked smug, but this time I didn't buy it.

"We should choose a song if we're going to have time to rehearse," I said.

He paused from taking his cock back into his jeans. "Really? You're going to insist we do this?"

I shrugged. "Yes, sir," I said with the slightest quirk of an eyebrow.

He pressed a hand to his forehead. "Fuck, you're going to be the death of me, woman." He actually looked amused.

What were the chances he would lighten up after this? Did I want him to? Maybe just a little.

"Big tough asshole like you?" I teased. "You can deal with it."

"I still really, really hate you." He lowered his hand and sighed. "Fine, but don't fuck this up for me.

If you do, I'm going to make you say *yes, sir* around my cock until you suck me dry."

"Noted," I said. I wasn't sure if he intended that to be a threat or incentive to screw up.

Whatever. If he wanted to threaten me with a good time, then I was here for it.

## 6

### PENN

I RUBBED my temple with my fingertips. "Jackson is fucking nuts if he thinks this would be ready tonight."

"He'd probably be surprised we actually agreed on a song," Abbie said dryly.

"Not as fucking surprised as I am." I thought she'd bitch and be difficult until she got her way. Apparently giving her orgasms lightened her up a bit. It should have done the same for me, but I was more on edge than before. Fucking her should have gotten her out of my system, but I wanted to touch her all over again.

Sitting beside her on my keyboard stool, I was very aware of her. She smelled intoxicating. Soap, shampoo, perfume. Whatever it was, I had to take shallow breaths so I didn't inhale too much. It was like a drug and I'd done enough of those in my life. Too much.

"Me too," she said. "I expected you to shoot down everything I suggested, just because I suggested it."

"I thought about it," I said unapologetically. "Pissing you off is fun."

"You need to get out more if you think being an asshole is fun," she commented. She toyed with the keys in front of her, smoothing her fingers over them rather than trying to make music.

I tried not to think of her touching my cock like that.

"I would suggest you try being more of an asshole to see what it's like, but you're already annoying enough." I resisted the urge to smile at the look on her face. I wouldn't be me if I didn't give her shit every chance I got. She gave back every drop of it and then some.

"Fuck off," she retorted. "You know, something occurred to me."

"You finally figured out why people don't wash coloured fabric with white?" I knew it irritated the shit out of her when I pretended I thought she was dumb. She was definitely not stupid. She might be one of the smartest people I ever met. Maybe I was lame for trying to get a rise out of her, just because I could, but I couldn't resist doing it every chance I got.

She poked me in the chest with a fingernail. "How the hell do the other guys put up with you?"

"I ask myself that every day," I said. "I guess they've learned to accept they will never be as hot and talented as me." I wanted to grab her finger and pull it, and the rest of her, closer to me so I could kiss her silly.

Instead, I batted her finger away.

"Are you going to tell me what occurred to you, or do I have to keep guessing?" I asked.

"I should keep you guessing, but since you're only going to come up with dumbass suggestions, I might as well come out and say it." She pressed down on the keys like she was trying to play chopsticks.

"Do you think Jackson really wanted us to perform together?" She dropped her hands to her lap and twisted around to look at me.

"That depends what you mean by perform." I didn't smile often, but I gave her a slight upward tug of my lips. Enough to show I was amused without looking happy. Let's not go too wild here.

She snorted. "Both meanings of the word."

I frowned. "You might have to draw me a picture, because I don't know what you're trying to say. You think he wanted us to fuck?"

A fascinating blush crept up her cheeks. For a woman who was very much *not* afraid of her own sexuality, there were still parts of her that held back, that were reserved but thankfully not embarrassed. No one should be embarrassed about sex.

I sure as fuck wasn't.

"Maybe not specifically that," she said slowly. "Think about it though. We've been hanging out for, what, three hours? And we haven't killed each other yet. He might have thrown out the suggestion just to get us to start talking to each other."

I scratched the side of my head. "That would be the kind of devious bullshit Jackson would pull. Levi too. This might have been some nefarious plot to try to get us to stop hating each other." Those two were all about team building exercises. I'd seen it tons of times with other bands. They even did those executive camp out week things.

I shrugged. "Shame it didn't work. We still can't stand each other."

I wanted to drag her down to the front of the stage and fuck her brains out in front of all the roadies who moved back and forth, getting every-thing ready for tonight's concert, but I still didn't like her.

No way. She was like the little brother's annoying best friend or something like that. She thought I was a shithead. I didn't plan to do anything to change her point of view.

Yeah, okay, I didn't believe it either.

"Of course we can't," she agreed. "But now we know we can spend time together without anyone losing a limb or an eye."

"Only because my cock didn't go anywhere near your eye," I said jokingly. "Something that big can cause damage." I placed a hand on my groin and wiggled it back and forth a couple of times. I didn't want to brag, but what I had was a good mouthful.

She laughed. "How many eyes have you poked out with your cock?" She glanced down towards it.

"None, but there's a first time for everything." I nodded. "If you're right about Jackson's motives, then I guess we can stop trying to practice."

"Trying to practice?" She frowned. "I was practis-ing. What were you doing?"

"Resisting the urge to grab a couple of Asher's drumsticks and poke my eardrums out every time you opened your mouth." I pushed the pile of sheet music in front of us into a pile and tapped it down on the stand to tidy it.

She rolled her eyes. "You're such an asshole."

"Did you just realise that?" I asked. "I thought you knew that since we met. I haven't been trying to hide it. Maybe I haven't been enough of an asshole if you haven't noticed."

She barked a laugh and turned to straddle the end of the stool. I couldn't see up her skirt, but the memory of the look and feel of her pussy was fresh in my mind. I wanted to push her skirt up and take another look, just to be sure my memory wasn't faulty.

"I noticed all right," she said. "I just think you're not as big an asshole as you try to act like you are."

"Hey." I pretended to be offended. "I'm a card-carrying member of the asshole club, thank you very much. A proud one." I left the whole being nice thing to Asher and Tully. They were better at it than I was, and seemed to enjoy it for some reason.

Ironic, since Tully was a trained assassin and Asher's family would kill you and not think twice. Zeke's family was worse. If there was a competition for the worst family, mine would still be in the running, just for different reasons.

"Keep telling yourself that." She turned around and swung her leg over the stool.

"I will." I nodded. I wasn't going to change for her or anyone else. Being brutally honest with people kept them at arm's length. I didn't want anyone getting close to me, because it just led to disappointment.

Usually theirs.

I had a lifetime of experience in not living up to people's expectations. Fuck doing that anymore. It was easier to let the music speak for me. If people didn't like that, then they wouldn't come to our concerts. And they did. Lots of them. Over and over.

"Can I ask you something?" She turned back around.

"Can I stop you?" I grimaced at her. If there was anything I knew about Abbie, it was that nothing I said or did would shut her up when she didn't want to be shut up. She didn't take any shit from anyone, not even me. I certainly gave her a lot of it. I vaguely wondered what it would take to make her really, truly angry. So angry she couldn't think straight. If it led to more amazing hate sex, then maybe I should try to push her to that limit. She hadn't complained about it. Yet.

"Nope," she said lightly. "That song, 'Lock Me In.'"

Every muscle in my body stiffened. No, not my cock, just everything else. I mean, my cock was an organ, not a muscle, but whatever.

Everything in me was on alert. That song was intensely personal and I didn't mind sharing it with the world, but I hated talking about it. It came up once in a while during interviews. They always want to know if it was about my past, my overdoses, my addiction. The whole fucked up mess. If you really want to piss me off, then ask about that time in my life.

"What about it?" I closed my eyes tight and braced myself for the barrage of questions I didn't want to answer. Would I answer them? I wasn't sure. I itched to get up and walk away, off the stage, right now. Walk and keep walking until I couldn't hear anything she said.

"Can I sing it with you?" she asked.

My eyes snapped open and then my brow fell into a frown. "You want to sing it with me?" Okay, I was *not* expecting that. "Why?"

"I don't know, I just...wanted to." She shrugged. "It's a beautiful song and it clearly means a lot to you. If you can handle my screeching, I thought it might be fun."

She knew it as well as I did that her singing voice

was not a screech. I could have listened to her sing all day. Maybe alternating that with listening to her come. Both were beautiful music.

I eyed her doubtfully. "This isn't where if we end up sounding so good together you insist we sing it on stage, is it?"

"Technically we would be singing it on stage," she pointed out.

I rolled my eyes at her. "You're such a mother-fucking smartass."

"Right back at you," she said. "So, how about it?"

For a good couple of seconds, I forgot she was talking about singing. All I could do was stare at the curve of her face, the colour of her eyes, the blush of her cheeks, the lines of her mouth. I wanted to kiss her so badly it was like an ache deep down.

More than that, I wanted to open up my heart and soul to her. I wanted to let her kiss and heal every wound, and push back all of the darkness until there was nothing left but me, laid bare and whole.

I forced my eyes away from her face. "Right. Sure. Just one more song. Then I need to eat, I'm fucking hungry." I hadn't finished breakfast and it was almost lunchtime. A big boy like me needed to keep up his sustenance.

"Hungry, yes," she sounded vague.

I wasn't sure if either of us were actually referring to food.

# 7

## PENN



"THAT MIGHT HAVE BEEN the best concert yet," Asher remarked.

"Yeah, it was okay." I shrugged and repositioned my feet on the chair in front of me. The view across Seoul from the roof of the hotel was beautiful. Especially since no one else was up here to enjoy it but us.

Thank fuck, because people splashing around in a pool behind me would be irritating.

I glanced sidelong over to where Abbie and Tully were snuggled up on a reclining chair.

Check that, they were making out.

I supposed the lead guitarist deserved some cheering up after having to kill his adoptive father. I tried not to watch too much when he slid his hand up her shirt and caressed her breasts.

It was nothing I hadn't seen them do before, but it felt different somehow. Like he was touching something that was partly mine.

There was no jealousy on my part, not really. It was like having the rest of the guys play a song I wrote. Or me playing on one written by them. They belonged to all of us in a way. As long as we didn't share Abbie with the entire audience.

"Are you all right dude?" Asher asked. "You seem weird tonight. Weirder than normal." He grinned.

"I'm fine." I tore my eyes away from Abbie and Tully, and looked back at the view. I sipped my beer and watched the lights twinkle.

"You're definitely off," Zeke said from the other side of Asher. "Usually you would have given him the finger for that."

Belatedly, I gave Asher the finger.

Zeke leaned over the drummer to peer at me. His eyes widened. "You and Abbie did it, didn't you?"

Asher snapped his fingers. "That's what it is. He's got that, 'Penn got laid,' aura about him." He actually seemed excited.

I shrugged. "What if we did?"

"We told you you would," Asher said, as if he'd

somehow won a prize by knowing I would want to fuck a beautiful woman. It wasn't exactly rocket science.

"Next time I see a trophy shop, I'll drop in and buy you one," I said sarcastically. "Would you like it engraved?"

"Yes please," Asher said, the grin never leaving his face. "She's amazing, isn't she? When did it happen? When you two were alone together before the sound check?" His eyes widened. "Did you fuck on the stage?"

"You sound like a fifteen-year-old boy whose friend lost his virginity and you need to live vicariously through him," I remarked.

"Hey, I do not," Asher protested.

Zeke chuckled. "You kinda do, babe."

Asher turned to him. "Don't tell me you don't want to know the answer too, because I know you do."

"I never said I didn't," Zeke said.

Both of them turned to me.

I rolled my eyes towards the sky. City lights and cloud cover meant the stars weren't visible, just an inky blackness. I wanted to lose myself in it.

"It's none of your fucking business, but no," I said eventually. "The stage was full of people at the time."

"So?" Asher asked.

My gaze slid back down to where Tully and Abbie lay. He'd rucked up her skirt—the woman did love her skirts—and had a couple of fingers deep in her pussy. Her eyes were closed but her lips were apart. Her expression was one of concentration and ecstasy. It was hard not to get hard seeing her like that.

On the other side of them, Channing and Landon were making out. They both had their jeans undone, cocks in each other's hands. At the same time, they were watching Abbie and Tully.

"Not everyone is an exhibitionist," I said. I didn't mind watching in a public place, but these days I preferred to keep my fucking in private.

Asher laughed. "Who are you and what have you done with Penn? I've seen you fuck groupies up against the tour bus."

"Then there was the time he fingered that make-up artist when we were supposed to be getting ready for a photo shoot," Zeke said.

"Yeah, Jackson wasn't impressed," Asher said.

"She was," I said smugly. Tiffany and I had been there several times before but not for a couple of years now. She was a nice enough woman, but she wanted to settle down and have kids.

I was definitely not the guy for that. Not with her, anyway.

"There's no accounting for taste," Zeke teased.

"Ain't that the truth," I retorted. "I was thinking that about you too."

"For the record, I'm adorable." Asher sat forward and pretended to fluff his hair.

"Yes you are," Zeke agreed. He leaned over and gave Asher a kiss on the mouth. At first, it was just a light kiss, but it quickly became deeper, until they looked like they might swallow each other whole.

The feet of their chairs scraped on the floor as they put their arms around each other and drew each other closer.

"That's my cue to turn in for the night," I said to myself.

I doubted anyone heard. I put my half-drunk beer down on the table and slipped away to the elevator that led down to our rooms.

A clock on the wall said it was one o'clock in the morning. I stripped off my clothes and stepped into the shower. I turned up the heat until it was just below scalding and let the water cascade over me.

I grabbed the bar of soap and ran it over myself, starting like I always did with the needle scars in the crook of my elbow. Some people liked to hide them,

to forget that part of the past, but I always acknowl-
edged them. They were a sign that past me was a
fucking idiot. I probably shouldn't be here right now.
I did a pretty good job of almost making sure I
wasn't.

That wasn't something I wanted to forget. If I
forgot, I might get complacent. And if I got complacent, I might give in to the cravings. Some days I
wanted to.

Badly.

If it wasn't for the band and the music, I might
have.

At times, the only thing that stopped me was
knowing how much I'd regret giving in. Climbing
out of that hole was hard enough the first time. The
second time would be more difficult and a lot more
public.

The fucking press would *love* to tell the world
about me screwing my life up again.

I didn't want to acknowledge it yet, but Abbie
was a vital part of that now too. The anchor that
kept me in place when I wanted the tide to wash me
away.

Of course, thinking about her got me hard again.

I put the soap back, placed a palm on the shower
wall and gripped my cock in my other hand. I

slipped my fingers and up and down my length while I pictured her on her knees, her mouth around me.

She probably felt hotter and wetter than the shower. Her pussy certainly did.

I pumped myself slowly at first, letting the pressure build bit by bit. I closed my eyes and got lost in the fantasy of her lips and tongue working me, while her eyes looked up at me. Watching me to be sure I liked what she was doing.

I doubted she could do anything I wouldn't like.

I imagined her here in this shower with me. Water rushing down her face, drenching her hair, shining on her breasts. The water trickled between them, sliding down her belly, down to the folds of her pussy. I wanted to pull her to me, to feel the slide of wet skin on wet skin, my mouth on hers. My cock slipping deep into her. Her moans of ecstasy through parted lips.

I rocked my hips and pumped myself harder. I heard the way she moaned in the corridor, and called me sir. Why that got me going, I don't know, but it fucking did.

Then and now. I wanted to hear her say it over and over again. Especially when I was telling her what to do and she was obeying me.

Fuck, that made my cock harder than ever.

I grunted as I came, spilling pearly cum over my fingers and into the cascade of water. In moments, it was washed away, down the drain. My hand was rinsed clean.

I slumped and let my cock slip out of my hand.

I should have felt at least somewhat satisfied, but for some reason I felt edgier than ever.

No, I knew the reason. My hand was not Abbie. There was no substitute for the touch of another person, however I felt undeserving of it. Honestly, I was pretty fucking undeserving most of the time.

I claimed to be an asshole, but I didn't always like being that way. It was a lonely way to live.

Chill out, I don't want any pity for it. No fucking way. I made my own bed. It was my fault if I had to lie in it alone. Let's be real though, most of the time I hadn't. For years, I shared it with whatever willing groupie was around.

There was always at least one.

Since Abbie came along, the groupies went away disappointed. Or with the roadies or whoever else was around. There was always someone willing to take what they were offering.

I turned the water to ice cold and rested my head on the tiles on the side of the shower. My skin protested the sudden change of temperature, but I ignored it.

Some people got cock piercings as a penance for doing bad shit, I tortured myself in different ways. Like leaving when everyone else was getting it on, on the rooftop. No one would have cared if I watched again. I even thought about seeing if Abbie would take my cock into her mouth. Would she have? Possibly.

But like I often did, I walked away instead. I was good at doing that. Running away and avoiding my feelings. I lost myself in things like drugs, music and groupies. One of these days, I was going to have to stop and face all of this shit.

That day wasn't today.

I turned off the water, grabbed a towel and wrapped it around my waist. I stepped out into the room as everyone else was filing through the door.

I ignored any looks of concern and changed into a pair of boxers, right there in front of everyone. If they wanted to look, who was I to stop them?

I caught a glimpse of Abbie in the corner of my eye, taking a good look while the guys hurried around, getting ready for bed.

I turned to face her just before I pulled my boxers over my cock.

She gave me a secretive smile that made my stupid heart do a somersault.

Did she have to be so fucking gorgeous? This would be a lot easier if she looked like a potato.

Hell, no it wouldn't. She would still have found a way under my skin, and all the other guys' skin too. It wasn't just about how she looked, it was her. She was smart, talented, sweet and badass, fragile and tough.

She had all six of us wrapped around her little finger, and she didn't even seem to know it. If she did, she wasn't conceited about it. She just...went on being her.

The woman I was not worthy of. Not in a million years. I asked myself how I was going to deal with her being in our lives, in my life, and keeping her at arm's length when all I wanted to do was touch her everywhere.

I had no answers for that, I just turned away and wished I had something stronger than alcohol to get me through the rest of my life.

## 8

---

### ABBIE

"Hey." I had to trot to catch up with Jackson, who seemed determined to avoid me since Singapore. Tonight's concert in Mumbai was the last on our Asian leg. I didn't want to leave the continent without getting some answers from him.

He paused mid-step right before the stairs that led up to the stage. His brow shone with sweat from the sticky, humid air.

I was starting to get used to it, but I'd had a lot of cold showers in the last few days to rinse off and cool down.

He turned around and looked at me with an expression that suggested he was distracted at best. Maybe he was busy and not avoiding me. He had a lot on his plate keeping two bands and a tour in line. That was a lot of ducks to keep in a row.

Not that we got too unruly. Most of the time.

"Is something wrong?" He massaged his temples with his fingertips. "Please tell me there's not another... *gift*. We're not about to come under attack again are we?"

He kept his voice down, but his brow creased. He certainly went above and beyond the normal duties of a band manager. Poor guy.

"No," I said quickly. "There haven't been any more *gifts*, thank God, and Zeke hasn't said anything about someone coming after us."

We hadn't even seen any sign of Hunter and Parker. Yet.

Jackson sagged slightly with relief. "Good. Any problems with the press? They seem to be behaving themselves for the most part."

"The occasional question about Vance's death, and Calista having been taken by a shark, but nothing I can't handle." I shrugged.

"Great." He made to step towards the stage.

"I wanted to ask about the duet you suggested Penn and I do," I said before he could move too far.

He stopped and sighed. "The one you both keep claiming isn't ready?"

"It isn't," I said with a faint smile.

"I haven't seen you rehearsing." He cocked his head at me like he thought I was trying to get away with something.

"Were you trying to push Penn and I together?" I said in a rush.

"Ahhh, that." He straightened his head.

"Yes, that." I crossed my arms over my chest, comfortable in the knowledge he was the only one who didn't stare at my breasts. At least, not that I noticed.

"He's been a lot less snarky with you lately," Jackson said. "I would like to see you perform together, but if all I get is a bit of peace and quiet between you, then I'll take it. That might be something to work out before the next tour."

I blinked. "The next tour?"

"Yes, well." He placed his hands on his hips and furrowed his brow. "Your tour, their tour, co-headliners, whatever. It won't be the same as this tour. Since you and the boys seem to be joined at the hip now, no doubt I'll be bitched at if you don't see each other once in a while."

"That would be nice," I agreed. I thought a lot about after, but it hadn't occurred to me Jackson might have thought of it too. It was nice of him, but I doubted it would be that easy. We would be told where to go and when, and we would go.

"So us not killing each other was a side-effect of you asking us to sing together," I concluded. "Not the main reason for it."

"Well," he said slowly, "that might have been a small part of it. Penn gets mad, and he's possessive of his solo."

"I noticed," I said dryly.

"At the end of the day, all he wants to do is make music." Jackson hesitated. "More than that, he doesn't just accept that he's talented and leave it at that. He's always pushing himself to get better. To write more complex songs. To push the boundaries. Working together was always going to be a challenge. For both of you. Once he realised that, he wouldn't have been able to resist doing it."

"You're much more devious than I realised," I said. He knew how to play Penn as well as Penn knew how to play his keyboard.

Those were some mad skills right there.

Jackson grinned. "Sometimes you have to be when you're dealing with temperamental rock stars. If you're not a step ahead, you'll be several steps behind."

"Tell me about it," I said dryly. "We are the worst." I didn't mind admitting I was just as bad as the rest of us. Okay, some of the rest of us. I would never demand peeled grapes or chocolate covered ants with gold leaf or any of that crap. But I had my moments.

"You're not so bad," Jackson said generously. "I've certainly managed worse. Of course, I've signed NDAs, so I can't give you any details, but you can imagine."

"I can," I agreed. "Like getting married for publicity."

He winced. "That was a crappy thing to do, but people have done worse things for publicity. Like have children."

"That *is* worse." I made a face. What a horrible way to come into the world. Especially if their parents treated them like a commodity.

Sometimes people sucked. Thank fuck neither Vance or Pete got me pregnant.

I tilted my head and gave him a speculative look. "Of course, now I'm wondering who you're referring to."

He snorted a laugh. "I'm sure you are, but I can't tell you. If you look it up on the internet, don't ask me to confirm or deny, because I can't do that either.

Besides, the kid doesn't deserve to be the object of conversation."

"That's true, they don't," I agreed. "It's sad what people think they need to do to succeed."

"Right." He nodded. "It would be nice if people were recognised just for their talent. This industry gets more cutthroat every year." He grimaced. "Sometimes literally. Sorry, that was a bad choice of words."

"You're not wrong though," I said. "Although, I don't think whoever is behind the *gifts* is interested in furthering their own career. Unless they have a very specific skillset and audience in mind." That was a twisted fucking idea right there.

"I don't think there's much market for those kinds of skills," he said. "At least, I hope not." He looked a little green, presumably at the memory of Poppy's head in the box.

Fair enough, it wasn't something anyone wanted to see every day. Well, not normal people.

I wondered if he knew about Tully's assassin training. Probably. There wasn't much that went on that Jackson didn't know. This wasn't the time or place to ask about it.

"I've kept you for long enough," I said. "I should grab something to eat before soundcheck."

He nodded. "We don't want one of our stars fainting from hunger."

"I certainly don't," I agreed. "I'll make sure they eat too." I knew he was referring to me, but I couldn't resist pretending I didn't understand.

He chuckled. "I'm sure you won't have too much trouble there. Some days, I don't know where they put all that food. If they're not careful, we'll have to roll them onto the stage."

I giggled. I knew what he meant. The guys did eat a lot. They burned it off on stage or exercising whenever they had the chance, but if I ate as much as they did I wouldn't fit into any of my clothes after a week or two. Well, unless I took up the drums as well as singing. Asher probably burnt off a big meal after only a song or two.

Jackson patted my arm and headed up onto the stage.

I watched him for a moment before turning and starting back to the green room.

Halfway there, a strange sound echoed through the narrow corridor. I stopped and frowned.

What the—

It was high-pitched and odd, but not unpleasant. If I didn't know better, I'd think it was some sort of child's plastic toy. That wouldn't be the weirdest thing to have happened since I met the guys, but it was still odd.

I stepped into the green room as one of the guys laughed.

It took me a moment to realise it was Penn. He was actually smiling. I hadn't realised until now he had a dimple in his left cheek.

How would I have noticed; he rarely smiled. He was even more gorgeous when he did. He actually looked relaxed and happy.

"It's gonna take more than that. Better luck next time." He tossed a plastic whistle onto the table in front of him. It was bright pink with holes down the top, and a mouthpiece. Exactly the kind of thing kids loved and parents hated.

Penn glanced up and saw me standing in the doorway. His smile evaporated and his expression shut back down to his usual scowl.

If I hadn't seen his smile for myself, I wouldn't have believed it. Not to mention the laugh.

"What's going on?" I asked awkwardly. I felt like I'd walked into a party I wasn't invited to. For some reason, that stung a bit.

Asher turned and grinned. "Everywhere we go, we try to find an instrument Penn can't just pick up and play. The more absurd the better."

"Fucker does it every time," Zeke said. He shrugged and picked up the whistle to give it a closer look before handing it to Channing. "This is more your thing."

Channing wiped the mouthpiece on his T-shirt and put the whistle to his lips.

The sound he made was closer to the one parents dread than the one Penn was making a minute ago. He grinned and tossed the whistle back onto the table.

I frowned. "Wait, you got an actual musical sound out of that?"

Penn shrugged. "Yeah."

"He can get an actual musical sound out of anything," Zeke said. "No practice, nothing. He just picks it up and plays."

"That's...incredible," I breathed. "I've heard of people who could do that, but I've never met anyone."

Penn looked smug. "I have skills. Something like that whistle is pretty basic, but the lip placement is different from the saxophone. Channing could do it if he played it properly."

Channing flopped down in a chair. "I'll stick to my sax. It's sexier than that thing anyway."

"Everything is sexier than that thing," Tully said.

He stepped over to me and slipped an arm around my waist. "Especially you."

"Thank you," Asher said as if Tully wasn't looking straight at me.

"You too," Tully said over his shoulder.

"So you guys search around for weird and wonderful instruments to try to catch Penn out?" I asked. "Including things like drums and harmonicas."

"Even castanets," Tully agreed. "And spoons."

"There was a beerphone once," Zeke said, referring to the instrument that was basically a stick with beer bottle lids nailed to it. "That was especially fun."

"Can you play a lute?" I asked Penn.

"Yep." He crossed his arms over his chest.

"Oboe?"

"Yes."

"French horn?"

"I've only tried once, but yes." He was completely unruffled.

"Violin?" Surely he couldn't have played everything, ever.

"Since I was four," he said. "You can stand there all day and throw instruments at me, but the answer is yes."

"It really is," Asher said. "At least in this, he is as good as he says he is."

"In every way, I'm as good as I say I am," Penn said.

I caught a flash of doubt in his eyes, but it was gone as quickly as it arrived.

"We'll keep trying to find something he can't play," Zeke assured me. "One of these days, we'll find something." He stepped to the other side of me and kissed my mouth.

"Good luck with that," Penn said. "In the meantime, don't we have a soundcheck to do? With real instruments."

## 9

---

### PENN


"I'M GOING FOR A RUN." I needed to burn off this morning's breakfast and a bunch of excess energy. Okay, and some frustration. At this rate, I would be more fit than ever. Was that mentally healthy? Probably not. Did I give a shit? Kinda. Whatever, I could run that off too.

"I don't know if anyone should go out alone," Zeke said as if he could actually stop me.

"It's India, it's kinda hard to be alone," I pointed out. Any of them could have come with me, but apparently an hour in the hotel gym this morning was enough for them. Whatever. That was their choice.

Zeke scratched the side of his head. "Okay, but be careful. Don't forget we fly out to London tonight."

"Yeah." I sat down and pulled on my running shoes. "Don't leave without me this time."

Abbie looked up from where she sat by the window reading a book. Some kind of hockey romance by the look of it. I could just make out the author's name, TB Mann, and a half naked guy on the cover.

"This time?" she asked. "They left you behind once?"

Asher snorted. "Penn is full of shit, as usual."

"We didn't leave him behind," Landon said. "He was running late and almost missed the plane."

"If it wasn't for Jackson telling them to wait, he would have," Channing said.

I shrugged. "Like I said, you would have left without me."

"We would have," Tully said. "But we didn't. You would have caught up with us, sooner or later." Like Abbie, the guitarist was nose down in a book. It looked to be the same series she was reading.

I might have to sneak a peek when no one was looking. Of course, I couldn't be seen reading romance novels, even though I did for my own enjoyment. Besides, they're a good way to learn what women really want. And I enjoyed the smut.

"I'll be back in an hour." I tightened my laces and

headed out the door. Even though it was still early in the day, the heat was sticky and oppressive. Just what I liked. The hotter the better. And if it wasn't stinking hot, then I liked it freezing cold, like my showers.

I chose a direction for no particular reason and started at a slow run. That was as fast as I could go here, dodging people and slow-moving vehicles. Like any city, some of the people moved like they had to be wherever they were going yesterday.

The other half moved like they were in a competition with a snail to see who could move the slowest. With the traffic this thick, most of them couldn't go much faster anyway.

I swerved around a moped carrying two people that was doing its best to weave around the traffic. The driver didn't look like they minded if they hit a couple of people on the way through.

"Watch where you're going," I called out after them. They probably didn't hear me over the sound of the traffic and their own engine.

I coughed on their fumes and slowed to a walk.

I liked the hustle and bustle of cities, but this one was almost too much. A person would either get used to it or get overwhelmed by it. I was glad we were only going to be here a few more hours.

I'd worked up a sweat by the time I reached a park where a group of guys, all dressed in white, were playing cricket.

It was a sport I enjoyed watching more than playing. Mostly because, believe it or not, I wasn't good at it.

Yeah, there are things I haven't managed to nail. Hitting a ball with a bat is one of them. I could catch okay, but I was better at running and tackling than swinging.

Of course, my asshole parents didn't let me play any sport where I might get injured. They saw dollar signs the moment I picked up my first musical instrument. A football injury would have put an end to all of that. So I played when they weren't around to see.

Yeah, I had a rebellious streak. Shocking isn't it? All I ever wanted to do was live my own life and make my own choices.

I never thought that was too much to ask. One day I might sit down and talk to them about why they thought it was.

I leaned on a low fence and watched as the bowler sent the ball flying towards the batsmen. The batsmen swung and hit the ball with a crack. He dropped the bat and started to run. A small audience cheered him on.

"Fancy meeting you here," a voice said to the side of me. "What a coincidence."

"It really is," a voice said from the other side of me.

I didn't flinch when Hunter Brantley appeared on one side of me and Parker Brantley on the other. It was inevitable they would pop up sooner or later. They were like the shit you just couldn't get off the bottom of your shoe.

"I don't believe in coincidences," I said. "Especially since you two have been following us since Perth. Or is it since Sydney?"

"I think it's fair to say a bit of both," Hunter said. "You know how it is. We go where we're told to go."

"Great." I turned around so my back was to the fence. "In that case, go away."

Parker chuckled. "As much as we'd love to, we don't follow your orders."

I rubbed my chin. I needed to shave, the stubble prickled my fingers. "Maybe you should. You might get into less trouble that way. Or cause less of it."

"Hey, that's not very nice," Parker said, with totally fake hurt that didn't make me feel bad at all.

"The last time we interacted with any of you guys, we helped you."

"We saved your asses," Hunter added.

"Zeke and Asher did that," I said. "You two dragged a dead body away." I didn't bother to keep my voice down. No one was close enough to hear us anyway.

"See, we helped," Parker said. He gestured over at Hunter, who nodded.

"By the time we were finished, they couldn't have implicated any of us. You're welcome."

I snorted. "Okay, whatever. What the fuck do you want?"

"Some respect wouldn't go astray," Hunter said. "But since we're not going to get that from you, we might as well get straight to it."

I didn't like the sound of that. These idiots had kidnapped Abbie twice and threatened her with rape. They helped us when it served their purpose, but they weren't friends or allies. They were a pair of dangerous criminals. I doubted there was anything they wouldn't do if their big brother, Reuben told them to.

If they wanted to idolise one of their brothers, couldn't they have chosen Zeke? He was the only reasonable one amongst them.

"Get straight to it then," I said. "I have things to do and places to be." Mostly a shower and packing for the evening's flight. If I was lucky, I might find a moment to talk to Abbie. If I was really lucky, we wouldn't talk.

"We heard you had a little problem back in the day," Hunter said. "One that could have killed you."

I shrugged as if I didn't know what they were referring to. "We all have problems once in a while. You both have one in that you can't think for yourselves. Shouldn't you both be in university, getting an education? Getting out into the world on your own? You might even find there's a better life away from Reuben and the rest of them." That wouldn't be hard, surely. As brothers went, Reuben was a shitty influence.

Yeah, okay, I was a pretty crappy role model myself, but I don't pretend otherwise. Reuben struts around like he's king shit.

Parker smiled, but it wasn't a pleasant expression. It was so chilling I had to force myself not to shrink back away from him. Or punch him in the face.

I wasn't going to let on how disconcerted they made me. Pricks like this could probably smell fear.

"We like curry," Parker said. "And your company. We often say that, don't we Hunter? No one is more pleasant than Beauregard. Can we call you Beauregard?"

"No," I snapped. Not even my mother called me that. Thank fuck. The other boys at school called me Pennington from day one. I can't remember when that became Penn, but it was a shit ton better than Beauregard. What were my parents thinking?

"Great," Parker said as if he hadn't heard me. "Reuben has been on us about getting Zeke to quit the band. I know, it's probably starting to sound like a broken record. We're a bit over it ourselves, to be honest." He sighed dramatically.

"Good, then tell Reuben to fuck off and get over himself," I said. "It's about time he gave it up." Way past time, frankly.

"Oh, he hasn't given it up," Hunter said. "He just wants us to put an end to it once and for all. Since Zeke won't break up the band, we'll have to."

I frowned. "What the fuck are you talking about?" I shook my head. "You know what, I don't care. You've wasted enough of my time with your bullshit." I took a step away.

Hunter grabbed my left arm, Parker the right, their fingers bruisingly tight on my skin.

"What the—" I jerked my arms back and tried to pull away.

They were surprisingly strong. Their grip was like a pair of clamps screwed down hard. The more I struggled, the tighter they became.

"We're not done, Beauregard," Parker said. He still sounded pleasant, like we were old friends having a chat about nothing in particular.

I hadn't ruled out the possibility he might be a psychopath. Both of them. In fact, it seemed pretty clear they were.

"Don't fucking call me Beauregard," I growled. I wanted to grab both of their heads and smash them together as hard as I could. It might knock some sense into them. Honestly, right now I might not feel bad if I killed them. They were a pair of screwed up little boys.

Hunter pulled something out of his pocket. A syringe full of something clear. "This won't hurt a bit."

I writhed and tried to break away from them, but the asshole pulled the cap off the needle. Parker held me tighter while Hunter slid the tip under my skin.

"Don't you dare," I snarled. Was I asleep and having a nightmare? If so, I wanted to wake up now.

The way the needle pricked my skin as it entered… I was all too fucking awake.

Hunter depressed the plunger and the clear liquid was forced under my skin and into my vein.

"Motherfuck—" The site went numb so quickly, I could guess what it was.

"Don't worry," Hunter said. "It's not enough to kill you, just mess you up for a little while. Embarrass the band. Make things a bit difficult. The press is going to have a ton of fun." They both released my arms with a shove and stepped back before I could knock them on their asses.

I whirled around to face them. "Stupid cunts," I growled. "You have no fucking clue."

A bit difficult? These guys were out of their fucking minds. They wouldn't just mess me up a little bit, this bullshit could end my career.

I presumed from the way they talked, they didn't know about the clause in my contract, but if anyone found me like this, it was over.

Fucking *over*.

Neither looked even slightly sorry. If anything, they seemed to find this whole thing funny. Like it was a game to them. Like trying to end my career was something they did for shits and giggles. Like injecting shit into someone's veins was a laugh. How did they even get their hands on it anyway?

Yeah okay, that wouldn't have been the hard part.

Shame they didn't get arrested and thrown in a cell for carrying it around. They could be another inmate's bitches for a while. I wouldn't shed a tear.

Parker smiled like we were friends or something, and they both stepped away. "We'll leave you to it. Maybe stay away from any bodies of water."

I muttered something that wasn't even coherent to myself. My vision was already starting to blur. I was feeling a strange combination of relaxed, euphoric and pissed off as hell. The anger faded though, blurring into the muddle of sensations like melting marshmallows.

Yum, marshmallows. Thinking about that made me feel like a marshmallow. Soft, squishy and boneless.

Marshmallows didn't have bones, right? What was mallow anyway?

What was coherent thought right now too? Who cared? Not me. I didn't care about anything right now.

I sat down on the ground with a flop and leaned my back against the fence. The crack of the ball and the roar of the crowd sounded strange in my head, like an echo being heard by someone else.

I blinked a couple of times, but everything made less and less sense. Something told me I couldn't stay here, but I couldn't remember why. I grabbed onto the fence palings and managed to pull myself to my feet.

Squinting against the glare—was it that bright before?—I started walking.

## 10

ABBIE

"It's been three hours." I put my book aside after realising I read the last paragraph three or four times.

"Long enough for a good nap," Asher remarked. I frowned at him and he shrugged. "I'm not wrong."

"I guess not. Aren't you worried about Penn?" I uncrossed my legs and sat forward in the chair.

"Usually I'd point out he can take care of himself," Zeke said slowly. "But it has been a long time, and with all the shit that's gone down recently..."

He picked up his phone from the table in front of him and pressed the screen.

Another phone rang from the vicinity of Penn's bed. The ringtone was one of the generic ones preprogrammed into the phone.

I would have guessed Penn would have something more interesting but that wasn't as strange as the fact Penn left without his phone.

Zeke pressed his screen again and shoved his phone into his back pocket. "I'm going to go and look for him."

"I'm going with you," I said. I gave him my best, 'don't try to talk me out of it,' face and he nodded.

"Fine. Asher, come with us."

For once no one made any jokes about sex. Evidently they were more worried than they let on. That immediately put me on guard. If anything got to them, it must be bad. Hopefully we were worrying for no reason.

"Tully, Channing and Landon, stay here and let me know if he turns up. Keep your eyes open."

We all knew what that meant. Zeke was expecting trouble of some kind. I didn't know what kind of skills Landon and Channing had, outside of playing bass guitar and saxophone, but Tully's skills would keep them safe if they had none of their own.

"Got it." Tully nodded. "He probably just got sidetracked at a strip club or something."

"Why would he need to go to a strip club when he has us?" Asher asked. When everyone turned to him questioningly, he grinned. "What? We're all hotter than any stripper I ever saw."

"No offence to any strippers, but you guys certainly are," I said.

"So are you." Asher slipped his hand into mine and squeezed gently.

Zeke opened the door and peered outside into the corridor. "It seems safe enough, but don't let your guard down. My lead singer senses are tingling." He flashed a smile over his shoulder.

"Do you also slay vampires?" I asked, mostly joking.

"I've been known to impale people from time to time," he said. He wiggled his eyebrows at me and pressed the down button for the elevator.

I laughed. "Yes. Yes you have." I put my other arm around him and leaned into him while we waited. After a minute or two, the elevator doors slid open and we stepped inside.

"Any other day, and I would distract both of you in here." Zeke sighed with undisguised frustration.

"We could always come back once we find Penny," Asher said. "I bet he's not too far away. He probably got lost. I would if I went out there without my phone."

"You'd be more likely to leave a lung behind than your phone," Zeke said.

"Hey," Asher said in protest. "Just because that's accurate doesn't mean you should come at me like that." He looked like he was struggling to hold back a grin.

"I'll come at you some other way later then," Zeke said. He leaned in to give Asher and then me a kiss on the mouth. "You're right though, he probably is lost."

"Is that what happened the first time?" I asked. "When you almost left him behind?"

They exchanged a glance.

"It's a long story," Zeke said finally.

"And it changes every time he tells it," Asher said. "I think the original version involved a redhead. Then it was twins. Then it was three, but they weren't related."

"I think those were two different times," Zeke said. He scratched the side of his head and led us out of the hotel and onto the street. "Penn—he used to get around. We all did. But that's in the past."

"None of us were celibate before we met," I said with a shrug. I didn't care what they did back then or who they did it with, as long as they didn't do it now. If they wanted other women, or men, then they could break up with me or each other first. I would sooner let them go than be cheated on. If they needed something that the rest of us couldn't give, then it was what it was. There was no point clinging to something that wasn't working.

"Okay, in a city full of millions of people, where could one keyboardist be?" Zeke mused.

"Is it possible he *is* in a strip club?" I asked tentatively. Did I have any right to ask that question? Just because he and I had sex and were almost getting along didn't mean we had progressed into relationship territory.

That may never happen. He was free to do whatever and whoever he wanted.

Asher and Zeke looked at each other.

Zeke shook his head. "It's never really been his jam."

"Brothel?" I ventured, trying to hold back a wince.

"Slightly more likely," Zeke agreed. "But not when dressed in running clothes. Any place like that he'd go into would have a better dress code than that."

I'd have to take his word for it. My knowledge of brothels was exactly zero. I wouldn't judge anyone for working in one, but I'd never been so needy for sex that I've gone to one. Not yet anyway. Hopefully not ever.

"Let's hope he didn't get run over." The traffic got thicker as we walked.

Although, it also got slower. If he was hit, he stood a reasonable chance of walking away with only a few bruises.

I didn't hear Zeke's phone ping, but he pulled it out of his pocket and frowned at the screen.

"What is it?" Asher asked. "Don't tell me, he got arrested for something? Let me guess, public nudity?"

Zeke glanced over at him, confused. "What? No. It's a tipoff as to his whereabouts." He looked pissed off.

My heart sank. "Please say it's not…"

"The evil twins," Zeke confirmed. "No explanation, just a location."

"Can we believe he's actually there?" I trusted the twins as far as I could throw them. Just thinking about them reminded me of the way they touched me. Hands slithering up the inside of my thigh. Pinching my nipple.

I suppressed a shudder.

"There's only one way to find out," Zeke said. "It's

not far. I'll send a message to Tull, in case this is some kind of diversion."

"What would it be like to have a normal family?" Asher mused.

"No idea," Zeke said. "My birth family and my present family are both insane." He flashed us both a quick grin, then tapped on his screen.

"Even normal families are a special kind of crazy," I said. Mine was pretty ordinary, in that they weren't involved in organised crime, that I knew of. But they were still a long way from perfect.

They hadn't had much to do with me since the first scandal with Vance. They gave me the old, 'we don't know what to say,' then said nothing. It could be better, but I got it. Sometimes there were no words to express how fucked up things were. Or how bad we felt about them.

Whatever. The guys were my family now.

"Stay close," Zeke said. He grabbed my other hand and we walked in a chain through the crowded streets.

People glanced at us in annoyance for taking up so much space, but I ignored them. Since the twins more or less confirmed their involvement in what-ever happened to Penn, I was a lot more wary and a bit more scared.

I was not letting either of the guys go. For all I knew, this was a distraction so the twins could get a chance to kidnap me again. I wasn't going to let that happen no matter what it took to stop it.

"It's just up ahead," Zeke said.

The streets emptied out onto a long, wide park. An unexpected splash of green after the greys and browns of the road.

Maybe a hundred metres away, a group of people looked to be packing up a game of cricket. It was a sport I knew very little about. As a kid, I was good at hitting a ball with a bat, but I couldn't catch for nuts.

I scanned the area. There were plenty of people here, but I couldn't see any sign of a six-foot-three, muscular keyboard player. Or a pair of six-foot-two, identical assholes.

"I'm starting to get a really bad feeling about this," Asher said.

"Really?" Zeke asked. "Because I've had a really bad feeling about this since we left the hotel."

"Yeah, well, I'm just catching up." Asher turned a slow circle, worry on his gorgeous face. "Do you think he would hear if we shouted for him?"

"We should have brought that whistle," Zeke said. "He'd hear that."

"Like a dog whistle?" I asked.

"No, one of us could play it really badly and he would get so irritated he'd come and punch us out." Zeke half-smiled, but his expression was laced with as much worry as Asher's.

"I could try singing really loudly," Asher said. "That would have the same effect."

"That would get you arrested for causing a public nuisance," Zeke teased.

Asher flipped him off. "I'm not that bad."

"No, you're not, so it wouldn't work anyway." Zeke pressed his fist to his hip and shook his head. "He's got to be here somewhere. Let's take a look around. Before anyone asks, we're not splitting up."

"I think I speak for Abbie and me when I say neither of us was going to ask," Asher said.

"Definitely not," I agreed. "I keep expecting your brothers to jump out from behind a tree or something." Not just the twins, but the other two I met as well. I assumed Reuben and Caleb were in Sydney and Melbourne respectively, but who knew what the truth of that was?

Zeke turned his concerned expression on me. "Fuck. I should have left you behind in the hotel with Tully. Asher could always take you back—"

"No he can't," I said firmly. "Firstly that would be the definition of splitting up. And you just said that wasn't happening. Secondly, I'm here now and I want to help. Thirdly, it was my choice to come."

Which then reminded me of how Penn made me wait before I came. I wanted to feel that again with him. I had to believe that whatever was going on, he would be fine.

I was going to be really cranky with him if he was dead.

Zeke held up his hands in surrender. "Fine. Let's look for Penn. Just…keep an eye out for the little pricks too. I would bet just about anything they're around here somewhere."

He didn't need to explain which little pricks he was referring to. Whatever ground they made up with Zeke by helping in Perth, they were losing if they did anything to Penn.

I wasn't sure if any of us would be able to stop him from killing them if he saw them again. I also wasn't sure if any of us would try. Penn was one of us. He was family. Even if he could be a massive pain in the neck.

We crossed most of the park before we saw the bridge. It spanned a narrow stretch of water which didn't look especially clean. It wasn't fast flowing either, which meant it was probably deep. The smell of it was certainly unpleasant.

I noticed all of that right before I noticed Penn. He was standing at the railing looking down at the water.

I raised my hand to point.

Before I could speak, Penn started to climb up onto the railing.

## 11

ABBIE

"Fuck." Zeke started towards the bridge at a flat run. "Stay together," he called out over his shoulder.

Hands clasped tight, Asher and I followed as fast as I could run. The drummer could have kept up with Zeke; I thought about telling him to, but I knew he wouldn't. Just in case this was a setup, he'd choose to stay with me.

Penn climbed higher. He reached the top and straddled the railing. He stayed like that for a moment or two before trying to place his foot on the thick railing at the very top. He wobbled dangerously and teetered over the water.

My heart stopped. Zeke wouldn't reach him before he fell. And when he did...

Penn windmilled one arm and wobbled back the other way.

My heart restarted but sat firmly in my throat. People were starting to notice what was going on. For the first time in I don't know how long, I didn't give a shit. There was so much more at stake than reputations. I didn't realise how much I cared about the grumpy guy until right now.

I opened my mouth to shout at him to get the hell down, and that I needed him, but Zeke reached before I got a coherent sound out.

Zeke growled and grabbed for Penn's leg. He missed the first time, when Penn wobbled again.

He swiped his hand back the other way and clamped his hand around Penn's knee. With a yank, he tugged the keyboard player back toward his shoulder.

Penn slipped sideways and tumbled, slamming into Zeke. Zeke grunted and they both fell with a thud of arms, legs and dust.

Zeke shoved Penn off him and stared, hands out to either side. "What the hell are you doing, dude?"

Penn rolled over and sat up. He looked confused. He blinked heavy lids over glazed eyes.

"Fucking hell," Asher muttered.

I murmured something in agreement. That was exactly what I was thinking. Worry gave way to frustration. What had he done? More importantly, why?

Penn pushed himself to his feet and staggered back towards the railing. "I can fly," he declared.

Zeke scrambled up and grabbed his arm. "No you fucking can't. If you go off that railing the way you are, you'll bloody drown." He glanced at us frantically. "We have to get out of here. Before anyone starts filming him."

Shit. I'd forgotten about the clause in his contract. If anyone pulled out their phone, videoed him and uploaded it to the internet, the whole band would be screwed. Especially him. There would be no coming back from that kind of broken loose hell.

"Could Jackson—" I started.

"Jackson can't do anything," Asher said evenly, but clearly unhappy. "Not in this case. He'd have no choice but to go straight to Levi. We have to deal with this before Jackson or anyone else sees him."

I nodded. That might be a big ask in a crowded place. A few people stood around watching, but if anyone recognised us, I couldn't tell. It was possible people tried to climb all over the bridge on a regular basis. Stranger things had happened.

Zeke pulled Penn's arm around his shoulder to support him. "Asher, get on his other side. We'll have to pretend he's drunk or injured and hope people buy it."

He looked furious. With good reason. Whatever Penn took, he could have put the whole tour in jeopardy. We might end up on a plane back to Sydney tonight, instead of London. Not to mention, Penn could have died. And for what?

"Personally, I'd be happy to beat the snot out of him to make it look more convincing," Asher said dryly.

"Me too," Zeke said with a grunt.

Penn jerked away from him. "What are you doing? Hey, why is there a bunny rabbit?" He squinted towards the ground a few metres in front of him.

"The bunny is telling you that you need to come with us," Zeke said with no hint of amusement. "You need to sleep for a while."

"No, I need to fly." Penn tried to turn back around.

"No you don't," Asher said. "Look, the bunny is hopping away. We need to follow it." He waved in the vague direction of the road.

"Follow the bunny," Penn said with a silly smile.

This might have been funny if it wasn't so bloody serious.

"Where are we going to take him?" I asked.

"No idea," Zeke admitted. "Somewhere quiet. Keep an eye out for anyone who looks like press. Or an evil twin."

He didn't need to tell me that. I was already looking. Anyone with a phone in their hand was suspicious, as far as I was concerned. As for the twins, I always had half an eye out for them anyway.

"I want to fly," Penn said miserably. "Don't care if I don't land."

"It's wearing off," Zeke said. "He always gets morose near the end."

"And then sleepy," Asher said. He patted Penn on the chest. "It's okay, buddy, we've got you."

Penn squinted at him. "Why?"

"I ask myself the same question," Asher said. "You're a pain in my ass but you're my brother."

"Pain," Penn echoed as if he couldn't quite understand the word. "Lots of pain."

We got him out to the street across to a narrow alley between two tall, skinny buildings. There was nothing in the alley but rubbish and a few sheets of cardboard that suggested people slept rough here from time to time.

The guys lowered Penn to the cleanest of them, so he was sitting with his back to the wall.

Zeke crouched beside him. "Why the fuck did you do this?" he growled. "Why now? You've been kicking ass for four years. Why today?"

He looked so disappointed, my heart hurt.

Penn screwed his eyes shut. "I didn't. It wasn't... Fuck." He shook his head. "Didn't want to."

Zeke snorted. "That's what they all say. It's all about the excuses."

Penn looked like he was going to cry. He started to stand but Zeke put a hand on his chest and shoved him back down.

"You can screw up your own life, but you don't get to screw up everyone else's. You need to stay here until you come down. If Jackson sees you high as a kite, you know what he's gonna do."

"Yeah, they knew," Penn said like a lost little boy.

"What does that mean?" Asher asked.

"They," I echoed softly. I crouched down on the other side of Penn. "They who?"

"There is no they," Zeke said. "Just like there was no rabbit. Like he can't fucking fly." He gave Penn a dirty look. "It's a hallucination because of whatever he bloody took."

"I don't know about that," I said. "Look at his arm." I put a hand over bruises that looked like finger marks in the crook of his elbow. Fingers that were bigger than mine.

Asher and Zeke both looked doubtful.

Zeke shook his head and opened his mouth to say something before he realised what I was getting at. "Shit."

"Penny," Asher said slowly. "Are you saying someone did this to you?"

Penn frowned. "They looked the same, but there was two of them."

"In any other context that wouldn't make any sense," Asher said with a sigh.

Zeke rubbed his forehead with his fingertips. "Are you saying the twins did this? Held you down and injected some shit into your vein?"

"Yeah." Penn leaned his head back against the wall and closed his eyes again.

"If that's a handprint, it's at the wrong angle for him to have done that to himself," I pointed out. "How else would they have known where he was?"

"But why tell us?" Asher asked.

"If I tried to make sense of what they do, I would

end up with a raging headache," Zeke said darkly. "It could be something as simple as Reuben wanting to remind us he could reach us whenever he wants to. He could have called all of the newspapers in Mumbai, but he *generously* chose not to."

He rolled his eyes. "This bullshit though—this is a new low. Messing with someone's addiction just to make a point is all kinds of fucked up."

"He doesn't need the press to know," I said softly. "Just Jackson. Would Reuben know about the clause?"

"The twins might not, but Reuben definitely would," Zeke said. "He makes it his business to learn things like that. People's weaknesses, so he knows how to exploit them. Still, he must be getting desperate to try this."

He flopped down beside Penn. "Whatever we do, we have to make sure Jackson never finds out." He pinched the bridge of his nose. "Shit, I hate lying to him, but we don't have a choice."

"If we can get Penn back to the hotel and into his bed for a couple of hours, we should be all right," Asher said. "Between us, we can distract Jackson long enough."

"If anyone can do it, we can," I agreed. I didn't bother to hide how appalled I was that any member of Zeke's family, or anyone else for that matter, would do this to another person.

Penn might be an asshole at times, but he didn't deserve this. Honestly, right now he didn't look like an asshole. He looked normal and very, very vulnerable.

I hoped like hell this wouldn't put him back on the path he'd worked so hard to get off. As far as dick moves went, this was way worse than what Vance did to me. Sticking poison into Penn's body... They could have killed him. What the hell were they thinking?

Were they thinking at all? The lengths these people would go to, to get their way was, frankly, terrifying. If they'd do this to Penn, they'd do anything to any of us.

*Anything.*

"Are you up to walking, Penny?" Asher asked. He stood and offered Penn his hand.

Penn looked confused for a moment, but took it. He was still clearly under the influence of whatever the twins gave him, but he wasn't as high as he was when Zeke pulled him off the railing. His eyes were no longer glazed, but he looked tired and not quite present.

While Asher pulled, Zeke gave Penn a shove to

his feet that was so hard the keyboardist staggered a few steps forward. If it wasn't for Asher's steadying hand, he would have plopped down on the other side of the alley.

With Asher supporting him on one side and Zeke and I following behind, we started the slow walk out of the alley and up the street.

"If he didn't do this to himself, then would Jackson—" I started tentatively.

Zeke shook his head. "He wouldn't risk it. Penn under the influence was too unpredictable. He would still have to tell Levi. Whether or not Levi would understand... It's just not worth it."

"They understood gifts in boxes," I pointed out.

"Those were problems they could deal with," Zeke said. "This... this better not become a problem again. We have enough of those right now as it is."

"It won't be a problem," Asher said over his shoulder. "We'll take care of Penn, even if we have to handcuff ourselves to him for the rest of his life."

"Yeah," Zeke said vaguely. Apparently Asher had more faith in Penn and the band than Zeke did right now.

I slipped my hand into his. "What is it? Is this just about Penn?" I suspected he was troubled by something more.

"This shouldn't have happened," Zeke said after a moment. "It's my fault for letting him go by himself. I should have made sure someone went with him, or that he didn't go at all."

"You couldn't have stopped him," I pointed out. Penn was determined to go. So hell bent on it, he'd forgotten to take his phone.

"I could have tried," Zeke insisted. "I could have gone with him. Hell, I could have had a tracker inserted into his right butt cheek."

I snorted a laugh. "I don't think that would have done anything. He still would have gone by himself, because that was what he wanted to do. He is as stubborn as they come. Like you. Like me. No one expected the evil twins to pop up and do some-thing...evil. How could any of us have predicted that?"

"We knew they were around somewhere." Zeke's mouth twisted to the side with annoyance. "They were probably waiting for one of us to be alone."

"Right," I agreed. "They could have given any of us whatever they gave Penn."

"PCP," Penn muttered. "That's what it feels like. Fucking bad shit."

As far as I could tell, it was all fucking bad shit,

but I would take his word for it that this was worse than anything else.

"It might have just been bad luck for Penn that it was him," I said. I hated to think what would happen if they did it to me. Or any of the guys. Just because the twins promised not to rape me didn't mean they wouldn't do other things while I was stoned off my head. I didn't know what. I didn't *want* to know, frankly.

"Lucky it wasn't me; I really would have sung," Asher said. He'd moved away a little, so Penn was walking on his own, but kept a hand out to catch him if necessary.

Penn walked with a slight stagger every few steps, but under his own power at least. He looked like he was ready to fall face-first onto the pavement. That made me angrier than ever. If I saw the twins again, I'd kick them both in the groin while wearing heels. Imagining the pain on their faces was more satisfying than it probably should be, but I was okay with that.

"Small mercies," Zeke muttered. He flashed Asher a smile when the drummer glanced over his shoulder.

"Zeke would have tried to play the drums," Asher said.

Zeke let out a short laugh. "I know better than to try. Those things are harder than they look."

"I like hard," Asher said.

"Me too," I couldn't resist saying. I hoped sneaking Penn into the hotel wouldn't end up being hard.

That was the kind of hard I didn't like.

## 12

ABBIE

IN THE END, no one paid us much attention. By that, I mean staff who work in hotels like the one we were staying in, know to look the other way, and not comment on what famous guests are up to. They might gossip later, but no one stopped to take any pictures or incriminating videos.

Zeke, who made a note of where the internal CCTV cameras were, led us through the foyer, making sure one of us was between them and Penn, even inside the elevator.

I found myself beside the keyboardist, our arms touching.

"Are you okay?" I looked up at his face. He looked like he'd been run over by half the traffic in Mumbai.

"What do you think?" He sounded more like himself. I wasn't sure if that was a good thing or not.

"I think maybe we should have let you fly," I retorted. It felt good to banter with him. I was grateful to the universe, fate or whatever that I could. No thanks to the twins, in spite of the fact we might not have found him in time if they hadn't told us where he was. If not for them, we wouldn't be in this predicament at all.

"You fucking would," he grunted. "I'm surprised you didn't push me."

"I thought about it, but Zeke got to you first." I shrugged.

"I thought about it too," Zeke said. "But that water looked dirty enough without you ending up in it as well. You would have polluted the crap out of it."

"Sounds about right," Penn said. He scrubbed his face with his hand.

"Zeke would have jumped in after you if you went in," Asher said. "And so would I."

"I would have looked after their shoes to make sure no one stole them," I said. "Assuming they had the sense to take them off before they jumped." Their shoes were expensive and would have weighed them down.

They both glanced at their feet.

"Priorities," Asher said. He looked back up and grinned. "You know what they say. Shoes before dudes."

Zeke looked at him sidelong. "Who says that?"

"I do now." Asher wiggled his eyebrows.

"That's the dumbest saying I've ever heard," Penn said from behind his hand.

"I bet it's not," Asher said. "There are some pretty dumb sayings out there."

Penn spread his fingers and frowned at Asher. "That's true." He closed his fingers again.

"I think we're doing a pretty good job of acting normal for the cameras," Asher said softly.

"It's not going to be normal in a minute," Penn said with a groan. "I need to get out of here. I'm gonna be sick."

We all took a step back away from him, which would have done absolutely nothing if he was sick. The elevator was tiny.

"Hold it in," Zeke ordered. "We're one floor from ours."

Penn lowered his hand. His face looked several shades paler than normal. "You know that's not how reflexes work, right?"

"Make it work," Zeke said in a growl. "Everyone is going to notice if you puke in here and on us. Let's not give Jackson a reason to request a drug test. Okay?"

"I'll do my best," Penn said. His face twisted in an uncomfortable grimace.

I put a hand on his arm.

Before I could say anything, he said, "If you're thinking of saying something sweet, don't. That really will make me sick."

"In that case, swallow it the fuck down or I'll kick your ass," I growled.

"That's better," he said. "It would be even better if you call me sir again."

Zeke and Asher looked at us both in surprise.

"What?" Penn asked. "Everyone has their thing. Why not me?"

Before anyone could say anything else, the elevator pinged and the doors drew open.

Saved by the bell.

We stepped out into the empty corridor and hurried to our room, all of us on alert for any sign of Jackson. Just to look at Penn, it was clear he was still affected by the drug. His face, his speech and the way he walked would all give him away.

Asher pulled out a key card and unlocked the door.

Penn was the first one inside, hurrying towards the toilet just in time to be sick.

"Is he okay?" Tully asked.

Zeke closed the door behind us. "He will be." He told the other three what happened in as few words as he could manage. They all looked predictably outraged.

"What the hell?" Landon asked. "Who does things like that?"

"People who had the needle broken off their moral compass," I said dryly.

I walked over to the bathroom door to make sure Penn wasn't going to pass out and drown in his own vomit. That would really top off an amazingly crappy afternoon.

He stood from where he'd knelt in front of the toilet and grabbed his toothbrush. He must have noticed my reflection in the mirror.

"What?" He started to vigorously brush his teeth.

"Just making sure you're all right," I said. "From one victim of the evil twins to another."

He spat. "No, I'm not fucking all right." He rinsed his mouth and put his toothbrush away. "I'm going to have a shower. You going to watch that too?"

"Is it an invitation—" I started to say.

I froze at the sound of knocking on the hotel room door. I twisted around to look.

It was Channing who peered through the peephole. "It's Jackson," he mouthed.

*Shit.*

I acted without thinking. I closed and locked the door behind me.

"I guess I am watching."

Penn's eyebrows twitched, but he quickly undressed and left his dirty, sweaty clothes on the bathroom floor. Evidently he didn't mind me staying around to look.

I didn't either. I especially didn't mind when he stepped under the water and it started to cascade down his body.

There were definitely worse sights in this world than hot, naked, wet rock stars.

"You could always join me," he offered.

I put up my hand and pressed my ear to the door. I heard the guys talking and laughing, but couldn't make out what was said. It didn't sound intense or like anyone was in trouble. Not yet at least.

"They're probably out there telling Jackson you and I are in here fucking," Penn said.

I turned back to face him. "Yes, chances are that's exactly what they're doing."

Whatever it took to throw off any potential suspicion. I hated having to treat Jackson this way after how well he looked after me and the rest of us. Even if Penn took the drug by himself, I wouldn't have wanted him to wear the punishment for a moment of weakness.

I was far from perfect. The mistakes I made almost cost me my career. I knew how he'd feel if the same happened to him. I would kick his ass into next week, and so would the rest of the guys, but we would have his back.

I tilted my head. "It's good to see you weren't adversely impacted for too long."

Steaming water rushed over his erect cock.

"You can't keep a good man down," he said smugly.

I snorted softly and closed the distance to the shower. I leaned in so he could hear me when I lowered my voice.

"You know you scared the crap out of us all, right?"

He leaned out until his nose was almost touching mine. "I wasn't fucking enjoying myself."

"You also know Zeke is not going to let you go anywhere by yourself ever again." I raised one eyebrow at him.

"He does the same to you and you don't seem to mind," he pointed out.

"Bad shit happens when we're alone," I said.

He smiled slowly. "Good shit happens when we're alone." He reached out with one dripping hand and tangled his fingers in the front of my shirt. He pulled me to him until his hot, wet lips found mine.

I stepped into the water, not caring that my clothes got drenched all the way through in seconds.

He pressed me against the side of the shower and kissed me like he was starving.

On some level, I suspected he realised if we hadn't reached him in time, he might be lying in that dirty water right now, not standing in hot, clean water. With hot, clean me.

He pulled back and his eyes me raked up and down . "That's a good look for you."

I glanced down at myself. Every centimetre of fabric was plastered tight to my body. It left absolutely nothing to the imagination.

"I seem to be overdressed for the occasion." With his help, I wriggled out of all the wet fabric and left it in a heap in the corner of the shower.

"Even better," he said. "Now," he tangled his fingers in my hair and pulled my head back far enough to kiss my neck, rough and with a grazing of teeth and stubble, "get on your knees and suck my cock." He let go of my hair and gave me a push down.

I didn't resist, but I did look up at him and smile. "Yes, sir."

He groaned. And once more when I circled his tip with my tongue. He gripped my hair again and held me in place while I teased him with my tongue on his cock and my hands massaging his hot, wet balls.

"Stop teasing and suck," he ordered.

"Yes, sir," I said, my words muffled by my tongue licking precum from the seam in his tip. I slipped my lips around him and took him in as deep as he could go. My eyes on his face, I started to suck.

He tilted his head back and groaned loud enough they undoubtedly heard it out in the room. At least we were being authentic. And having fun doing it.

"Good girl," he said breathlessly.

For some reason, his words made me hotter than the shower water. I wasn't really used to that kind of praise, but I liked it, especially in this context. If he wanted to be the dominant partner and me the good, obedient partner, then I was here for it. It was arousing as fuck.

I closed my eyes to keep out the water when it

brushed across my face, and sucked like his cock was the most delicious thing I ever tasted. It was certainly right up there. At the same time, I kept a gentle pressure on his balls, caressing and massaging in time with my sucks.

"Fucking hell, woman, your mouth feels even better than I imagined," he ground out.

I opened one eye and looked up at him, wondering how many times he'd imagined this. More than once by the sound of it. I was glad I lived up to his expectations. There would be nothing worse than being told I give a bad blowjob. Although, according to most guys I knew, there was no such thing.

He gripped my hair tighter and I knew he was close to coming.

I opened the other eye and watched the ecstasy on his face. The shower and now this, seemed to have washed away most of the effects of the drug. He was certainly not as sluggish as I might have expected.

Anything but.

He looked down at me. "I'm going to come in your mouth."

I nodded as best I could with a mouthful of cock and sucked a little harder.

He grunted and his hips pumped him deeper and deeper into my mouth. Finally, he let out a low groan and squirted hot cum into my throat. He held me there and panted for a while until he caught his breath.

Finally, he managed to say, "Swallow it."

I was intending to do just that, but I pulled my head back from him, locked my eyes on his like I had when I sucked off Tully in Perth, and swallowed down every drop. It was tasty, mercifully with no hint of any strange, illicit substances.

"Good girl," he said. He reached out to pull me to my feet. "Let's get dry." He traced a finger lightly around one of my nipples, making me shiver. "It's time for bed."

"Do we still hate each other?" I asked as I stepped out of the shower and reached for a towel.

He smirked. "Definitely."

"Good." I started to dry myself. "I would hate to think anything's changed."

## 13

### PENN

"Are you getting enough sleep?" Jackson squinted at me critically. He didn't look like he thought anything suspicious was up. If anything, he seemed amused, like Abbie wore me out. Which was accurate.

"Not today," I said lightly, as smug as I could. My head was pounding like a jackhammer. All I wanted to do was to curl up under a few blankets with a couple of painkillers and a cup of coffee.

The last thing I felt like doing was boarding a flight. The couple of hours of sleep I got after giving Abbie three orgasms wasn't nearly enough.

Thank fuck by the time we got out of the shower, Jackson was gone. By the sound of it, he made a quick escape so he didn't have to listen to any more groaning.

I have to give Abbie credit for saving my ass. And blowing me off. The woman's mouth was next level perfect. She put my imagination to shame.

Yeah, I sighed mentally. Fucking her was better than being on stage. I was in big damn trouble now. Was it healthy to trade one addiction for another? Probably not. Did I care? Nope. She was better than any drug.

"I'll sleep when we get to London," I said. "Or on the plane." Or both.

He gave me a hard, companionable clap on the arm, just missing the bruises and puncture wound covered by my shirt. "You do that." He got up from his seat and moved across the boarding lounge to where Violet sat with her guys.

"He's like a mother hen sometimes," Tully remarked. He slipped into the chair Jackson vacated and handed me a cup of coffee.

I nodded my thanks. "He got me worried he suspected something, but I think he just wanted to catch up on the gossip."

Tully chuckled. "There's plenty of that going around right now." He glanced over to where Abbie sat between Asher and Zeke, and smiled.

"You don't think this is weird at all?" I frowned lightly. "All of us guys and one woman?"

"Have you ever worried about what other people thought about you?" he countered. "Outside the band, I mean. I know you care what *we* think." He gave me a lopsided, ironic smile.

I snorted. "I don't give a shit what anyone thinks. This thing could get ugly if it falls apart. What if she decides she doesn't want one of us?"

"Are you scared she'll reject you?" He opened the lid of his coffee and took a sip.

"Hell no," I lied. "It's more likely I'll get sick of her. Then I'll have to put up with her being a pain in my ass while she hangs out with you clowns."

"You weren't complaining too loud when you had your face between her thighs," Tully said. "It's good to see, and hear, you making progress with each other."

"Pervert," I said. Of course, we were on my bed, in the middle of the room, in full view of everyone.

"Same to you," he said with no hint of shame. "You seem to enjoy watching."

"I do." I shrugged. It wasn't as much fun as taking part, but there were worse ways to pass the time. Like sitting in an airport, waiting for a plane, while your brain tried to burrow out of your skull.

I sipped my coffee and enjoyed the way it burned down my throat. "Have you thought about what comes next?"

He cocked his head at me. "You know me, I like to live in the moment. Let the universe figure out what's going to happen from here. Are you worried about something in particular?"

He sounded like my therapist.

"After the tour," I said. "When we all go back to our more or less individual lives." We spent a lot of time together, probably more than was healthy, but Abbie changed things. We were becoming more than a band, more than brothers. We were becoming a polyamorous group. All the guys with Abbie and then two pairings within that. Wherever we went from here, things would be different forever.

This could either be amazing or end up a massive shit storm.

Tully nodded. "Okay, yeah, I wonder about that too. Zeke and Asher were practically living together before. Landon and Channing too. Both of us live pretty close to them. Maybe nothing changes, and maybe we buy a mansion and all live in it together, I don't know."

He paused for a moment, then added, "I'm surprised you're the one asking these questions. You seemed to be the most resistant to...all of this. I know it's not really because you think Abbie is a pain in the ass." He looked at me over the rim of his cup.

"Are you sure about that?" I asked.

He grinned. "One hundred percent certain. She's the least pain in the ass person I've ever met."

"Except for me," I said jokingly.

He laughed. "Right, yes. Except for you." He rolled his eyes toward the ceiling and grinned.

"Sarcastic bastard," I muttered.

He looked unapologetic. "How are you feeling anyway?" He glanced over to make sure Jackson wasn't listening.

"Like shit," I said. "I can't believe I used to do that on purpose. It's not worth it." Then again, people always said that when they had a hangover yet they still drank alcohol. No one ever said humans made sense. Most of us were dumb as fuck.

"So, no chance of backsliding then?" he asked pointedly.

I honestly didn't know how to answer that. I didn't become an addict on purpose. No one did. At the time, I needed something to help me deal with life. I didn't realise how bad it got until I overdosed the second time. In retrospect, it was fucking obvious, but at the time it wasn't. It crept up on me like a spider, then bit me in the ass.

"I don't want to," I said finally, honestly. "It's the last thing I want. It's screwed up enough having to sneak around and lie to Jackson when I didn't do it to myself."

Stupid as it might sound, I didn't want to see the look of disappointment on our manager's face. If the guys were like brothers, then Jackson was like a father. More than my biological father was. Or like an uncle. Jackson gave a shit. He was a good guy. A better guy than me. Like that would be hard.

Tully nodded. "Good. If you ever feel like you might, you know you can talk to any of us, right? We'll be more than happy to hold you down and kick your ass if we need to."

"Thanks," I said awkwardly. "I think." Their support was a major factor in me getting through the last couple of years, but I wasn't sure if I could, or would go to them if the cravings got too bad. I was used to dealing with that shit by myself. Which was basically the problem in the first place. Me and my stupid, fucking pride.

"You're welcome. I mean it, bro. We're family. If we don't look after each other, who will?" He gulped down the last of his coffee.

"You're not gonna try to kiss me are you?" I asked. I held my arm up in front of my face.

"Nah, you're not my type," he said lightly. "I prefer cute, blond and female."

"I'm cute," I protested. "I'm definitely not the last two." Confident that I was safe from his lips, I lowered my arm.

He grinned and shook his head at me. "Yeah, you're adorable."

"Is that sarcasm again?" I asked. "Careful dude, you know how fragile my ego is."

He laughed so loudly I winced.

"Dude. Go easy on my brain."

"Sorry, dude, but your ego is not even close to being fragile." He looked like the least sorry person I ever saw. Asshole.

"Says you," I retorted. "I keep shit bottled up."

"Now that part is true," he agreed. "Except when you're writing songs. Then you let it out."

"Are you going to become a therapist when you give up guitar?" I asked dryly. "I feel like I'm being psychoanalysed right now."

"Maybe I will," he said with a shrug. "People are fascinating."

"That's a matter of opinion," I said. "I find most people annoying."

"I've noticed." He barely contained a smile.

"Is this where you tell me I should try to be more tolerant?" I asked. "Because fuck that. People should be less annoying." After a moment, and in a bid to change the subject, I asked, "How are you? These last couple of weeks have been a bit shit for both of us."

He sighed. "Yeah, I'm okay. My mother called while you were out. She's upset, but I got the feeling she had a fair idea of what happened. Not the exact details, but what he was up to."

"Not minding if you ended up collateral damage?" I asked. That was some crazy, messed up stuff right there. My parents sucked, but I didn't think they wanted me dead. Hell, even Zeke's family cared if he lived or died. Of course, he couldn't go back and play the dutiful son if he was a corpse.

Tully looked down at the floor. "Yeah. I think she was surprised I answered the phone."

That knocked the breath out of me for a moment. "Shit," I said softly, once I could form the words. "That's fucked up."

He looked back up and blinked away a glaze of tears. "It could be worse. I could actually *be* dead."

"With your ninja skills? No way," I said with certainty.

Zeke and Asher were kinda scary and had scary

families, but if I was really going to be afraid of anyone, it would be Tully. If he wanted to, he could kill me and I would never see him coming. I tended to do my best to stay on his good side, just in case.

He smiled faintly. "Even with ninja skills, I can be outnumbered."

"Not with the rest of us around," I said. "Whatever happens, we've got your back just like you've got ours." I offered him a fist bump.

He accepted, then went in for a bro hug. "You guys are the best."

"Hell yeah we are," I agreed. "Don't you fucking forget it either." I patted his back awkwardly.

"How could I forget it? You're always reminding me," he teased.

"You guys are so cute together," Asher called out.

I turned to see him grinning at me and flipped him off. I think he lived in some shiny little fantasy world where we would all couple off like a little package, with Abbie right in the centre.

If I was into men, it might be someone like Tully, but I wasn't. Unfortunately for Asher's fantasy, I wasn't going to fuck him to tie up some kind of imaginary loose end.

"At least we can have a fine bromance," Tully said.

"I can work with that," I agreed. Tully was easy to

like, compared to most people. That is, he was some-what less annoying.

That bar was pretty low though.

"Would you believe me if I told you I was worried about you earlier?" he asked.

"Nope," I said lightly. "You know me, I always pop back up sooner or later."

I could easily have *not* popped back up. I didn't want to admit it, but I was worried about myself as well. I still was. There was only a very small chance anyone would want to pull any of us over for a drug test, but that shit would be in my system for days. The longer it was, the less chance people would believe the truth. The bruises on my elbow would fade. The needle site would become one of many similar scars. Just because it was the truth didn't mean anyone other than the guys would believe it.

I'd be figuratively holding my breath for the next couple of weeks at least. And thanking fuck I wasn't some kind of sports star. There was no way in hell I would avoid a drug test then.

"I'm going to the toilet then going to buy a couple of books," Channing declared.

I looked over as he stood. Landon was frowning at him. He looked comfortable stretched across a few chairs, reading the same book Tully read the other day. It must be good if he was into it too.

Zeke swivelled around in his seat. "Not by yourself, you're not," he said. "What did I say about that?"

"The bathroom is just there." Channing pointed to a door maybe ten metres away. "And the bookshop is right there. You'll be able to see me the whole time." Before Zeke or anyone else could protest, the saxophonist jumped up and hurried across the room to the toilet.

I exchanged glances with Tully and shrugged. Even after what happened to me, it was hard to keep us in line. Channing was right though, we would be able to see him and there were lots of people here in the airport.

What could go wrong?

Yeah, famous last words.

# 14

## ABBIE

"HEY." Violet dropped into the chair beside me when the guys went to stand at the window to admire the planes. "It's like they never grow up, isn't it?"

I watched as Asher and Landon talked enthusiastically about some kind of aircraft. They all looked the same to me. Two wings, engines and windows. As long as they could fly, I didn't really care.

Zeke stood near them, looking about as interested as I was. Tully was deep in conversation with Penn, who looked exhausted.

I surprised myself by how scared I was for the keyboardist, but he made up for it with his tongue on my clit. He knew how to play me perfectly there too.

I laughed softly. "I guess it is. From what I've heard, growing up is overrated anyway."

"That's funny, I've heard the same thing." She sat back and crossed her legs. "How is it that we're on the same tour, but I hardly get a chance to talk to you? I've been meaning to see how you were after what happened in Perth. That shit got crazy, didn't it?"

"That's one word for it," I agreed. An understatement, but it didn't matter what you called it. We were lucky to get out of it in one piece.

"I'm okay, but thanks for asking." I gave her a quick hug. Honestly, I'd been meaning to check up on her too, but between the guys and work, I'd been too busy and distracted.

"Thank goodness things settled down after that." She pulled out a block of chocolate from her bag and opened it before offering some to me.

I broke off a row and took a bite out of it. "Thank you. Settled down, yeah."

I resisted the impulse to look over at Penn. Things had settled until today. For half a moment, I thought maybe all the shit would leave us alone. Forever would be good.

I should have known they wouldn't, but no one

saw what the twins did coming. Of course not, who would guess someone would do something so horrible, much less anticipate it? What's the expression? 'You can't make this shit up.'

"Just between you and me, I'm really looking forward to the European leg." She bit into her own row of chocolate. "I like that we get to travel in tour buses and cars instead of flying everywhere. And the scenery is just gorgeous." She drew the word out. "It's one of my favourite parts of the world."

"Mine too," I said. "Although, we'll see most of that out the bus window."

People thought touring was glamorous, but it was mostly a blur of locations and faces, and working. Not so much sightseeing and going to parties.

I wouldn't change it for anything.

"True, but looking out the window is pretty awesome," she said. "And meeting new people. I'm always up for doing that." She glanced around. "I've heard you're getting along well with all of the guys these days."

"Are you asking for gossip?" I teased.

She gave me a cagey look. "Maybe just a little bit." She held two fingers half a centimetre apart. "I mean, six guys is pretty impressive. I'm busy enough trying to keep up with four and we're not even, you know, fucking."

I felt my face heat a little. "I'm not sleeping with all of them." Yet.

Landon and Channing made it clear they wanted to, but the opportunity hadn't arisen. So to speak.

Of all the guys, I knew them the least. I'd have to remedy that at some point soon. Right now, I was still coming to terms with the fact Penn and I were finally starting to form a relationship. If you could call it that. I was ninety-nine percent certain he didn't hate me. I didn't hate him either, even when he was being an asshole.

"Oh?" Violet asked. She gave me a sidelong look. "What does that mean? Only one or two of them? Let me guess, Zeke and Asher?"

"Well, yes," I agreed slowly. "And Tully." After a moment I added, "And Penn."

Her eyes widened. "*Girl*." She drew the word out slowly. "You're my hero. We need to find time to have drinks so you can tell me all the details."

"All the details?" I echoed.

"If I can't live the dream, at least I live it vicariously," she said.

She must not have noticed the way Blaise, Ryan, Sharkey and Danny looked at her. Even Blaise, who had a bigger chip on his shoulder than Penn, as far as I could tell, looked at her like he wanted to gobble her up. She could have them all eating out of the palm of her hand if she wanted to.

"I'd certainly like to find time to have drinks." I could agree to that much. I wasn't sure the guys would appreciate me sharing details of our sex lives, even with her. Okay, some of them wouldn't mind, but I might.

"There's something else I'd like to talk about," she said.

I frowned. "That sounds ominous."

She shrugged one shoulder and looked suspicious as fuck. "It might be."

She waited just long enough that I started to worry, then said, "I was hoping we could sing together. Actually, I was kinda hoping I could convince you to join Blazing Violet, but I don't think Wolf Venom is going to let you go any time soon."

My frantically racing heart slowed and I blinked. "Okay, I did not expect you to say that." She made my head spin. "You're right though, the guys probably wouldn't, unless you want to be their support act until the end of time." At least that way we could tour together.

She laughed. "Fuck no. Next tour, it's our time to

shine. In the meantime, I'd love to do a collab. Maybe we could write a couple of songs together and throw them on our next album?"

"I'd love that," I said sincerely. I found myself looking at her through a haze of tears. I fanned my face.

"Sorry, it's been a while since anyone wanted me to work with them." Levi hadn't really given the guys a choice. Before that, people didn't want to risk their reputations to work with me. Yeah, it sucked, but I got it. There's a fine line between doing anything for publicity, and tarnishing your image with someone the whole world seemed to love to hate.

"You know I'm me, right?" I pulled out a tissue and dabbed at my eyes before I ruined my mascara.

Violet snorted. "That's the best thing about you." She paused for a moment. "Look, I have to admit, when we heard you were touring with us, I thought it was a mistake. A publicity stunt." She winced apologetically.

"But then I met you, and I realised you're the bomb. The good kind of bomb," she added quickly. "You're one of the most genuine people I've met in this industry. Yeah, I know, it's a low bar sometimes. Watching you perform, I've learnt a lot from you.

And behind the scenes too. I think we can make amazing music together."

"I think we can too," I agreed. "Thank you for being honest with me. I thought all of those things at first as well." It hadn't occurred to me to wonder how she and her band felt about me tagging along. Granted, I had a lot of other things on my mind at the time. It was nice to clear the air before it became a problem.

"You guys have all been so welcoming. It's made a world of difference to how this all could have gone." If they treated me like shit, like Penn did at first, the tour would have been a nightmare for all of us. Especially me.

"Most of the acts at Onyx Riot Records were in it for themselves, even when we collaborated. Everything had to be their way or not at all. They hated to share the spotlight with anyone. Except Vance." I grimaced. I didn't like saying his name. "Touring with him would definitely have sucked." Not in the good way.

"Pete encouraged us to work together, but you know how it is." I didn't like saying his name either. "Musos and their egos."

"Let me guess, someone always acted like they

were the star and the other person was a backing vocalist?" Violet asked.

"Basically," I agreed. "The amount of backstabbing at that place was next-level ridiculous. I guess that will change now." Tully wasn't ready to think about it yet, but he'd do a great job running a label. And if he didn't want to, I wondered if he'd thought about merging Onyx Riot with White Wolf Records.

If anyone could handle the extra workload, it was Levi. Or rather, he'd know who to delegate it to. Jackson maybe.

"Anyway, I would love to collaborate with you," I said sincerely. "I can't wait. You, me and Candy in the recording studio sounds like the dream team." I couldn't suppress the excitement that passed through me. The experience would be incredible. Would I be able to convince Penn to play keyboard?

For the first time, I almost looked forward to the tour ending. Things would change, yeah, but now I had something amazing to look forward to.

I spent a lot of time listening to Violet's music over the last few weeks and just her suggestion of working together gave me so many ideas about how we could blend our styles.

Violet grinned. "Great. I can't wait either. They

might as well book a spot at the number one on every chart in the world for at least a year."

I grinned. "They're going to have to mine for more platinum."

She laughed. "Yes! They definitely will. Multi-multi-multi-platinum. Were all going to need really strong walls in our houses to hold up the plaques."

"I'm going to need a house," I said.

My bank account was a lot healthier now than it was the night Zeke and I met. I could almost afford to buy somewhere decent now. But how would that work? Would I invite the guys over for a night each? No, that wouldn't work for Landon and Channing. I wasn't sure it would work for Zeke and Asher either. I could give them two nights each, but then the other guys might be pissed.

I suspected the whole world wouldn't agree if I suggested we went to eight day weeks, just for my convenience.

Although, I had a compelling reason for it. Right?

Violet sat up a little higher in her chair. "I'm happy to help you find a place if you need it." She slumped back down. "But I guess the guys would want to do that too."

"I could use all the help I could get," I said firmly and with sincerity. "I'd probably choose a place that's about to fall down around my ears because I don't know what to look for. Or I'd fall in love with how pretty the tiles in the bathroom are, and not notice how dysfunctional the kitchen is."

"A functional kitchen is only useful if you actually cook," Violet pointed out.

I grinned. "That's true. Still though, I might learn how at some point. Or I could hire a cook. It would suck if they told me they weren't going to work for me because my kitchen was shit." It felt nice to have a silly conversation like this with another woman. Or anyone, really. Everything got so intense so often lately.

Death and chaos tended to have that effect on people.

"If they won't cook for you, then they'll have to take you out to dinner," she reasoned. "But if you insist, I'll make sure a functional kitchen is on the list. Between all of us, we'll find the perfect place for you. How many bedrooms do you need? I'm thinking—four?" She gave me a sly smile. "Or one really big one?"

I started to answer, but then had to stop and say, "I'll have to think about that. There's a lot of conversations I have to have and things I need to work out."

Things that got more complicated the more I

thought about them. At some point, the guys and I would have to all sit down and talk. I had no idea what they wanted and they probably had no idea what I wanted either.

I mean, *I* didn't know what I wanted. No, that's not true. I knew what I wanted but it might not be what the guys wanted. I hoped like hell we could figure it out so we were all happy. Was that too much to ask?

I didn't think it was. After everything we went through, we deserved some peace and contentment. And a huge soundproof room where we could practice together. And a cuddle puddle where we could watch movies. And—

Yeah, my dreams were bigger than my bank balance could manage right now. I might have to dial it back a bit. Or a lot. Maybe forget the cuddle puddle. Although, a home recording studio would be pretty fucking cool.

Violet nodded. "You know where to find me when you need someone to talk to and help with that. And anything really. Us girls have to stick together after all, right?" She offered me her pinky finger, which I took with mine and shook it.

"I don't think I've done that since I was about seven," I said with a laugh.

"You need to live a little," she said. "Everyone should pinky shake at least once a week."

"What was I thinking?" I threw up my hands. "Clearly I've wasted all of those years."

Violet giggled. "It sounds like we have some catching up to do then. When we get to London, I'm buying us all water pistols. Then I'm going to drag you all out somewhere for a water fight."

"If you're not careful, I might learn to have fun," I warned her.

"You should definitely have fun," she said. "We all should."

She opened her mouth to add something, but whatever she was going to say was interrupted by a man's shout of alarm.

I shot up in my seat. What the fuck?

I exchanged glances with Penn. He looked about ready to crap his pants.

A couple of security guards came running from some other part of the airport. Instead of stopping at us to grab Penn, they bolted past us and skidded into the men's toilets.

"I have a feeling they didn't just need to pee," Violet said.

The crowd outside the facility was growing.

Murmurs passed through them, both worried and horrified. What the hell happened in there?

I caught a glimpse of Zeke, his expression intense, eyes scanning the area. I didn't need him to tell me what he was looking for, or who.

Where the hell was Channing?

## 15

ABBIE

"Fucking hell," I muttered.

I pushed myself up out of my seat and stepped over to Zeke's side. "Do you think—"

He shook his head and spoke with a tightly controlled voice. "I don't want to think it. I need to go and look."

The security guards were trying to move people on from the area.

"It's too late for an ambulance," one of them said, his expression grim.

I put a hand over my mouth. "Oh God," I whispered softly.

If something bad happened to Channing... I couldn't finish that thought. Didn't want to. Like Zeke, I had to see for myself. "I'll come with you."

"Me too," Landon said. He looked terrified, his face pale. He and Channing were practically joined at the hip. If anything happened to him the one time they weren't...

Zeke looked at us both, then nodded. "Fine, but stay close to me. And keep an eye out for identical felons."

Any other time, I would have laughed at his description of his brothers, but there was nothing funny about this.

My heart heavy, palms sweaty, I walked across the boarding lounge with a gorgeous but scared rock star on either side of me. It took me a couple of moments to realise Asher, Tully and Penn weren't far behind.

"I'm sorry, you can't go in there," one of the security guards said.

Zeke looked like he was ready to shove the man out of the way. "One of our party is missing. We heard something bad happened to someone in there and we're worried it was him." I would have been convinced if I was one of the guards. Zeke was charismatic, even when times were desperate, like now.

The security guard must have had a stone cold heart, because he wasn't budging. "I'm sorry, sir, you'll have to wait for the ambulance to arrive." Judging by his composed tone, he was used to dealing with people like us, and situations like this. Emergencies in general, not dead bodies in particular, I hoped.

"Is someone helping him?" Zeke demanded. His face was red, eyes full of barely contained frustration. He'd looked less angry when he pinned his brother, Caleb, to the wall in Melbourne. He was clearly struggling to keep from lashing out.

The other guard looked apologetic, but unmoved. "I'm sorry, sir, he's beyond help." He didn't elaborate. He didn't need to. His simple words told us everything we needed to know.

My heart sank. For the second time in half an hour, I blinked back tears. This was seventeen kinds of screwed up. What the hell happened in there? I kept expecting the evil twins to appear and have a chuckle over their latest escapade. If they did, the next ones dead around here would be them.

"Fuck," Landon said softly. "I should have gone with him. Why didn't I?" He let out a whimpering, moaning breath.

I laced my fingers through his and lowered my head to his chest. I felt his heart racing.

Or breaking.

"I'm sorry, sir," the first guard said again. "I have to ask you to step back, away."

Reluctantly, Zeke waved us back a couple of steps. He looked like he was ready to lose his shit. Landon too. The rest of the guys looked gutted and lost. The guards could tell us to move away all they wanted. We couldn't, wouldn't, go too far, not until we knew for certain.

I sniffled and held back tears.

"You guys look like you're at a funeral," Channing said. He approached us, a smile on his face, a pile of books under one arm and a chocolate bar in his opposite hand. "What's going on?"

With a choking sob, Landon threw his arms around him. "Thank fuck. We thought you were dead."

Channing had to tighten his grip on his books to stop from dropping them, but he managed to get his other arm around Landon.

"Why would you think that? I told you I was at the bookshop. I've basically kept you guys in sight the entire time."

"We couldn't see you," Zeke growled, but he patted Channing on the back. "I watched you go into the toilet, but I didn't see you leave."

"You were looking out the window at planes."

Channing shrugged. "I was fine."

"This time you were," Landon said. "I shouldn't have let you go by yourself." He looked miserable.

I doubted he'd ever let Channing out of his sight again.

"Hey," Channing said gently, "we talked about this. We agreed that five or ten minutes apart once in a while wouldn't hurt. I'm fine, you're fine…and you still haven't told me what's going on out here."

Landon quickly filled him in.

"We're all accounted for," Zeke said. "So is Violet and her guys."

"I haven't seen Jackson for a while," I pointed out softly.

Zeke froze, but then nodded tightly. "I'll try him. If it's him in there, we'll hear his phone ring."

He pulled out his and tapped on the screen.

I held my breath and waited.

No ringing came from inside the men's room. Just a voice from inside Zeke's phone.

He put it to his ear. "Where are you?" He listened and nodded. "Okay, just checking. No, nothing. Everything is fine. Yep, see you in a minute."

He mashed his finger on the screen. "Jackson is getting a sandwich."

"Great," I said, my tone hollow. Not so great for

the family of whoever actually died.

"Yeah. We should go and sit down again. The plane should be ready to board soon."

It couldn't leave soon enough as far as I was concerned. I loved India, but enough bad things had happened today that I just wanted to get out of here.

This was getting to be a bad habit. Needing to get out of a country, or off a continent before something else happened. I wasn't looking forward to leaving Europe at the end of that leg.

"So you were worried about me, huh?" Channing seemed to have surrendered the other half of his chocolate bar to Landon and was now teasing him as they walked back to the chairs, their arms around each other.

"They're cute, aren't they?" Asher asked. He wound his arms around me and I stepped in closer to absorb his warmth and comfort.

"Very cute," I agreed. "You're all cute."

"Especially me," Penn said as he walked past us and flopped back into a chair.

"Especially all of you," I said firmly.

"But really especially, especially me," Tully said with a grin.

I shook my head at him. "Don't make me change my mind."

His smile softened. "As if you would."

With Asher holding me firmly to keep me from falling, I leaned over to kiss Tully lightly on the mouth. "Don't tempt me."

"I will tempt you every chance I get," the guitarist said unapologetically. "As will the rest of us."

"One hundred percent accurate." Asher pulled me back and slanted his mouth across mine for a tender, but heated kiss.

"They aren't wrong," Zeke said.

"Nope, they aren't," Penn said, his eyes on his phone screen. "We'd all fuck you right now if we could."

That statement made me feel as hot as hell all over. Any more of that and I would have to change my panties before I boarded the flight.

"Fact," Asher said. "If the men's toilet wasn't out of commission…"

I wrinkled my nose. "Yeah, hard pass on doing anything in there right now." I looked over to see a couple of ambulance officers arrive, pushing a gurney. They didn't look like they were in any particular hurry. I supposed they wouldn't be if, as the security guards said, it was too late.

They wheeled the gurney past the security guards and disappeared.

"Rather them than me," I whispered.

Asher shrugged. "I hate to say it, but when you've seen a few dead bodies, it stops bothering you after a while. They've probably seen hundreds of them."

I grimaced. He was probably right, which didn't make me feel any better. It wasn't something I wanted to become desensitised to.

I turned around in Asher's arms, so my back was pressed against his chest. I watched the crowds go by.

Some of them hesitated and stared at us. A few gave me envious looks. Others just got excited to see Wolf Venom in person in the airport. A few took photos before moving on.

I saw Jackson coming back from the kiosk, sandwich in hand, coffee in the other. I was pretty sure he drank more coffee than the rest of us combined.

He started towards us when the ambulance officers pushed the gurney out of the men's room. One of them was just pulling the sheet over the poor victim's face and head.

Jackson stopped mid-step, frozen, and stared. I could almost feel the heart pounding in his chest.

I frowned. "What the fuck?" Whatever it was, he looked as rattled as hell. It wasn't one of us. Maybe it was an evil twin. Could we be that lucky?

He shook his head and hurried over to us, the stunned expression on his face not changing.

"What is it?" I asked when he got close enough. "You look like you saw a ghost."

It took him a moment to respond. "It was Pete Rossi," he said in a hoarse whisper.

My heart stopped. "What the hell? I thought you just said..." I must be hearing things. Surely he'd only caught a quick glimpse?

"I did," he said. "The former owner of your old label. From the look of it, he hit his head." Jackson looked slightly pale. At least he wasn't running to vomit. Yet.

If it wasn't for Asher holding me, I would have hit the floor. I shouldn't have been surprised. I really shouldn't. Pete was the last in the line of people who screwed me over before I met the guys. If whoever killed them was going to go after anyone else, Pete was an obvious choice.

"Are you sure?" I said. My head spun.

"Yeah, it was definitely him," Jackson said regretfully. "I've met him several times before."

"Holy shit," I breathed. Was this really happening or was it yet another bizarre nightmare? I forced a few breaths in and out and tried to clear my head.

"I presume they think it was an accident," Asher

said lightly. He didn't sound anywhere near as shocked as I felt.

"Accident, my ass," Zeke said. "At least this time there's no chance of them trying to pin it on us." He rubbed a hand over the back of his head. "I hope."

"It's a little cleaner than a gift in a box," Asher agreed. "And the local authorities get to do the cleanup instead of us." He sounded very cheerful about that.

For some reason, that irritated the shit out of me.

"Yeah, those are the important things," I said sarcastically. "Let's not worry about the fact he's dead." I stepped out of the circle of his arms and turned to glare at him.

"Abbie," Zeke said softly. "You can't be freaking out right now. Freak out later, when we're alone. If you do it here, people will notice."

I wanted to shout at him but he was right. At some point, people were going to realise Pete and I were in the airport at the same time and wonder at the coincidence. Why was he here anyway? Had he followed me?

That was a chilling, sickening thought.

I closed my eyes and sucked in a deep breath. "Fine, but I will freak out later."

"Noted." Asher drew me back to him again and

tucked me against him, under his chin. "We'll freak out with you, if you like. Or hold your hand. Whatever you need."

"Thanks." My voice was muffled by his shirt and pecs. "I'll think about that."

He traced circles around my back with his hand, soothing me like I was a child.

"There has to be some explanation for why he was here, and what happened," Tully reasoned.

Zeke shrugged. "He was obsessed with Abbie. Wanted her back. Followed her around Asia and met his end with a nasty accident. If I had to guess, I'd say he has a ticket to London on his phone. He might have been looking for an opportunity to get her alone, but never found one. He seemed like the persistent kind."

I reluctantly drew my head back from Asher's chest. "He was. I just… I was starting to think this shit had stopped. I hoped it had."

Asher gave me a squeeze and nuzzled his face into my hair. "Maybe it has now. There's no one else left that's pissed you off. Except…" He lifted his head and looked straight at Zeke.

"The evil twins," Zeke finished for him.

# 16

## PENN

"Hello, London!" Zeke said as he stepped from the luggage carousel to the main entrance area to Heathrow airport. He strutted in front of us like he was on stage.

People stopped to stare and a few even clapped.

"Don't encourage him," I muttered. I caught Tully's gaze and rolled my eyes toward the ceiling.

Tully grinned. "He just really, really likes London."

"Yeah, who the fuck doesn't? He doesn't need to announce it to the world." I stopped to look back at two gorgeous women who were staring at me unashamedly.

"Oh my God, he's even better looking in person," one of them said.

I responded with my trademark smirk and kept walking. Yeah, okay, maybe London was all right. At least the women here had good taste.

Those two anyway. Plenty of them were staring at the other guys instead. And just as many were staring at Abbie, although it was mostly guys doing that. As for the beautiful woman herself, she walked in the middle of us like a queen, Zeke in front of her, Asher behind. Tully and I were on one side, Channing and Landon on the other.

She had her chin raised like she didn't give a fuck if anyone was looking at her not. I wasn't fooled though. I knew that little twitch in the side of her mouth, the way her eyes blinked a little faster. She liked the spotlight as much as the rest of us, but the spotlight had screwed her over and left her uneasy at times. It was bullshit. She should bask in it like the rest of us did. If anyone said anything bad about her, I might punch the shit out of them.

After sleeping most of the way here, I was feeling a lot better. My head still ached slightly, but it was a tolerable level. I had enough energy for a good right hook.

"I think there's a couple of people in London who didn't know Wolf Venom have arrived," Jackson remarked as we headed to the sliding glass doors at the front.

"Isn't it your job to make sure everyone knows we're here?" I asked.

He looked at me sidelong. "Yes, well." He cleared his throat. "The last couple of people who didn't know, now do, thanks to Zeke."

"Right, got it," I said.

We stepped out of the front doors into a media shit storm. For maybe a fraction of a millisecond I thought they were there for all of us, as they should be.

That was until they started to shout, "Abbie! Abbie! Did you know your former lover was found dead a few hours ago? Did you see him in Mumbai airport?"

Fuck.

She froze like a groupie caught with a mouthful of cock.

"I beg your pardon?" she asked the closest member of the press. In this case, a man I suspected was from a trashy magazine. "Vance died weeks ago."

And the acting award goes to Abbie Hart. She looked genuinely confused.

Frankly, I suspected she didn't fully believe Pete was dead until now. Jackson *had* only caught a quick glance. He could easily have been wrong about who it was.

Just quietly, I was glad he was right. This Pete guy sounded like a total prick, a shitty businessman and an even worse lover. Not to mention potentially stalking Abbie. If it wasn't him, it would have been some random dude who might have been a decent human being. If any of those existed. Naw, better that it was Pete.

"Not your former husband," the journalist, if you could call him that, said patiently. He gave them the impression he thought she was stupid. Asshole. "Your former lover. Pietro Rossi."

Abbie blinked even more rapidly than before. "Pete is dead? How? What the heck happened? I had no idea. Are you sure?" Her luscious lips dropped apart in shock.

Tully and I stepped in to grab her when she started to look like she might faint. She was turning it on for the cameras now.

"Yes, I'm sure," the sleazeball journalist said. "It's been announced officially."

Abbie shook her head and leaned against me, her face on my chest. Her own ample chest heaved as she drew in several thick breaths.

"So it's just a coincidence he died in the airport at

the same time you were there?" someone else called out.

"Okay, enough," Jackson said. "We're getting out of here." He bulldozed his way through the press pack to the van, which was waiting for us. He slid the door open and waved us inside.

Zeke climbed in first, then turned to help Abbie before the rest of us followed.

"Fucking vultures," I said as I was getting in. I made sure to be loud enough so they could hear me. Lowlife, bottom feeding, blood sucking leeches.

Yeah, I really hate the tabloid press. I wished they'd leave us alone and let us live our lives.

Instead, they excuse themselves by saying they're just doing their jobs, but it's a shit job. They should do something more useful with their time than follow celebrities around like a pack of hungry dogs. Like inventing a fitted sheet that folds up the way it came out of the packet. How hard could that be?

"Tell them how you really feel, Penny," Asher said. He patted me on the shoulder as I slipped into the seat beside him.

I shrugged. "Okay." I raised two fingers to the press as the van pulled away from the curb. "Is that eloquent enough for you?"

Jackson scrubbed his face with his hand. "You should probably not antagonise them like that."

"How would you like me to antagonise them, then?" I put my hands on the button of my jeans as though I was just about to pull them down and moon everyone out the window.

"How about not at all?" Jackson suggested. "I know that doesn't sound like much fun, but they did confirm what I saw."

"Yeah." That brought me back to earth.

I looked over to Abbie, who sat opposite me. She was looking out the window with eyes as glazed as mine must have been when I tried to climb up on that bridge railing. "You okay?"

It took a moment for her gaze to turn to me. "I don't know," she said softly. "I think I'd convinced myself it wasn't him after all. Or that maybe he was alive and the ambulance guys got it wrong. Or something."

I nodded and leaned over to put my hand on hers. "I know it's fucked up, but we'll get through it."

She nodded. "I know we will, it's a lot to deal with. After…" Her eyes flicked to Jackson and back to me. "After everything that's happened, I wish it would stop. You know?"

Yes, I sure did know.

"Yeah," I said simply. "Hopefully it's over now." Whatever happened to all the people who died, they were all easier targets than Zeke's evil twin brothers. Those two little cockroaches would be a lot harder to kill, even if someone was willing to piss Reuben off by trying. Even I wasn't dumb enough to want to get on the wrong side of big brother Brantley. He was a mean ass dude.

"For what it's worth," Tully said, his eyes on his phone screen, "while we were in the air, the police looked into what happened to Pete. They've ruled it an accident." He raised his eyebrows and looked up at Abbie.

"What?" she asked.

"He had a ticket to London and then one to every other city on the tour," Tully read from his screen. "And a bunch of photos of Abbie on his phone. Some from different locations in Asia, including one taken inside the airport. According to this, they are looking into his involvement with the death of Vance, Calista and Poppy Newton. Sounds like you had an obsessed fan. Apparently they believe he slipped on a puddle of water and hit his head on the sink. Nothing more than that."

"Fuck," she said softly. "He was following me around?"

"Can you blame him?" Asher asked lightly. "Personally, I would follow you anywhere."

I gave him a funny look. "Dude, do you realise how fucked up that sounds?"

He shrugged. "I didn't mean it in a weird way."

"That was how it sounded," I said.

"It was a bit weird, babe," Zeke told him.

"I would follow you too, babe," Asher told him.

They shared a quick kiss while I made gagging sounds at them.

"These guys stalking you aside," Tully said slowly. "I'm glad we made sure you're not alone for the last while. If he was the one doing the killings, then who knows what he might have done to you?" Even with the seatbelt on, he managed to get his arm around her. She leaned into him in a way that made me slightly envious of him.

Only slightly though, because I am obviously better looking and taller than him anyway. And I can play his guitar at least as well as he can.

Abbie shuddered. "I guess it's true what they say, you never really know someone, but he seemed so normal. Although…"

"Although what?" Jackson prompted.

"Even before he signed me with his label, he made no secret of the fact he wanted to sleep with me," she said. "Sometimes I wonder if that was why he signed me at all."

"That's bullshit," I snapped. Even when he was dead, the motherfucker was making her feel bad about herself. He was a piece of shit, dead or alive.

"I'm with Penn on this one," Zeke said. "He signed you because you're talented. End of story." He gave her a look as though daring her to argue.

"Zeke and Penn are right," Channing said. "And I don't say that very often. Especially that both of them are right. It's one or the other…" He cleared his throat. "Anyway, you are as talented as the rest of us. It's not okay that he was sleazy and made you feel that way."

"Right," Asher agreed. "If he wasn't dead, I would punch him."

"I would punch him anyway," I said. "Dead or not."

They all looked at me funny, but I meant it. If anyone laid a hand on Abbie, I would hurt them, even if they were dead. Okay, I didn't give a shit if that made no sense. It was what it was.

"It's probably lucky you didn't get the chance," Jackson said. "I have a funny feeling Levi wouldn't take it very well. I know I wouldn't."

"Not to mention those security guards would

have been pissed," Asher said. "Shit would have gotten ugly." He nodded like he was suddenly the wise guy of the group. Wise ass, more like it.

"It wouldn't have helped anything," Abbie said. "Except you getting arrested."

She didn't need to add anything about me getting drug tested, I saw it in her eyes, and knew it myself anyway.

"I'm starting to think I should put you all on one, long leash," Jackson said.

"Did you just suggest tying us all up?" Asher asked. "Because I might just be here for that." He grinned and wriggled his eyebrows.

"TMI," I said.

Jackson leaned forward, pinched the bridge of his nose and shook his head. "Remind me again why I wanted to manage you guys?"

"Money?" Landon suggested.

"Our good looks?" Channing said.

"Our personalities?" Zeke said. "Except Penn, who doesn't have one." He grinned at me teasingly.

"Fuck off," I said. "At least my personality isn't over the top with glitter on the side."

"That pretty much sums up the rest of us," Asher said. "The glitter part in particular."

"Only you guys would take an insult as a compli-ment," I said.

"That's not true," Tully said. "You do the same thing."

"I feel so attacked right now," I said with a dramatic sigh.

"Poor baby." Abbie leaned over to pat my knee.

I grimaced. "You didn't call me asshole." I didn't want to be called baby. At least, not in that context. I was supposed to be a badass rock star dude, not a marshmallow.

Asher leaned over and patted my other knee. "Poor asshole."

I grunted. "That's better. Don't forget it and start thinking I'm nice or some shit."

"Never," Asher said. The smile he gave me said otherwise.

Fuck, I was going to have to work harder or I would lose my asshole card.

## 17

ABBIE

THE MEDIA CONTINGENT around the hotel was even bigger than the one at the airport.

Jackson gestured for the driver to wait and let the van carrying Violet and her guys pass us. All the while, he was tapping on the screen of his phone, his brow creased in a frown.

"I'm going to have to talk to them, aren't I?" I pressed myself down as low as I could and let the wall of muscle that was Wolf Venom be my shield. I didn't want to hide behind them, but they were all drawing themselves up taller and sitting around in their seats so I couldn't be seen anyway.

"Absolutely not," Jackson replied. "Levi has his assistant putting together a statement." He read off his phone screen. "You're horrified to learn that your former lover was following you. You're shocked that he might have played a role in the deaths of several people. Your condolences go out to their families. You'd like it if you could process all of this in private and focus on the continuing tour. Which you have no intention of withdrawing from. You urge people to seek help for any mental illnesses."

"That sounds accurate," I said. "Nothing about his death?"

"We could say you're saddened by it, but that contradicts your response to his potentially being a stalker," Jackson said. "We can't exactly say you're glad he's dead because you're safe now. That wouldn't go down very well."

I snorted softly. "Not so much." I wasn't sure how I felt about him being dead, but I couldn't say I was happy about it. Was I sad? Not exactly. Mostly, I was conflicted because, in spite of the things he did to me, I thought he was a decent human being. Clearly that was all wrong.

"This isn't a gag order," Jackson said. "Levi won't ban you from speaking to them if you want to, but he'd prefer you didn't. As far as he is concerned, the matter is closed. You need to concentrate on work now. He's going to fly out in the next day or so to catch up with us. Read—check up on you and make sure you're okay. All of you."

I caught Zeke glancing at Penn and hoped Jackson didn't notice.

"All of us?" Zeke asked.

"If Pete was killing people, any one of you could have been next," Jackson pointed out. "Or me." He glanced around the van. "I see by the looks on your faces that hadn't occurred to any of you."

Penn grunted. "We're all harder to kill than that."

I looked over to see him gazing out the window. It didn't take a genius to understand what he was thinking. If Pete happened to see him when he was high, he would have been easier to kill.

Zeke cleared his throat. "Lucky for us, we're all fine. I suppose there's no point in telling Levi not to come out here?"

"Levi will travel to Europe using any excuse he gets," Jackson said.

"So it's not just about us," Tully said.

"I can neither confirm nor deny." Jackson smiled slightly.

We drove past Violet's van, which was parked in front of the hotel. She and the guys were getting out and greeting the press.

At a brief glance, the journalists weren't interested in Blazing Violet. They waved at our van as we slid past, but we were driven around the back and let into a gated area. The gate was shut and locked behind us.

"It's nice of Violet to run interference for us," Asher said. "We owe them one after that."

"Yeah, we do." I picked up my bag from where it lay at my feet, and pulled out my sunglasses. They wouldn't do anything to disguise me, but they'd reduce the value of any photos the press took through the gate. That wouldn't deter them, but I was fucked if I was letting them get rich from this.

Jackson opened the door of the van and I was herded out in the middle of the guys. I lifted my chin and pretended nothing was amiss, while trying to ignore the shouts of the journalists who had run around the back to see us there.

"Fucking vultures," Penn muttered. This time, he didn't stick his fingers up at them, and he didn't moon them either. He ignored them the same as the rest of us.

"Can we throw our suitcases at them?" Asher asked jokingly.

"I'd like to see you throw one over that fence," Zeke remarked. "Think you can do it? A full suitcase."

Asher turned to appraise the fence in question. "Absolutely, but it might damage the suitcase."

"There is no way in fuck you could get a suitcase over that fence," Penn said scathingly. "And you say I'm full of shit."

Thankfully several hotel staff came out to take our suitcases inside for us, before anyone tried throwing any of them. None of the staff gave us more than a brief glance. No doubt they were used to celebrities staying there and having to deal with crap from the press.

"I could, but I'm not going to try," Asher said. "Although, Penn's suitcase is a good size." He eyed it as a man dressed in the hotel uniform rolled it past.

"Touch it and I'll throw *you* over the fence," Penn growled.

"Hands up who wants to see Penn try that." Landon raised his hand.

Asher batted it back down. "Dude, that wouldn't end well for anyone. Mostly Penn, because he'd hurt himself trying to lift me up."

"Unlike Asher, I'm not dumb enough to try something like that," Penn scoffed.

I turned and shook my head at them. I was going to suggest they be nice to each other, but then realised banter was their attempt to take my mind off things. All of our minds. Unfortunately, it was going to take a lot more than that.

We hurried inside and followed Jackson and a concierge to the elevator and up to our rooms. In this case, two adjoining rooms with a door connecting them. A door that would probably stay open most of the time. None of them seemed to like to take their eyes off me for too long. Would that change now Pete was dead?

Presumably not, especially while the evil twins were still a threat.

"I'll leave you to it for a while," Jackson said. "I need to get Blazing Violet settled and make sure all the tour staff got into the country. You're on your own for the rest of the day. I suggest ordering in for meals and alcohol. And don't trash the room." He said that last with a smile.

"When have we ever trashed a room?" Asher asked with mock hurt.

"Never, but there's a first time for everything." Jackson pointed two fingers at his eyes, then pointed them at Asher before he stepped out the door and closed it behind him.

"Talk about being attacked," Asher complained.

I slipped off my sunglasses and shoved them back in my bag. The hotel rooms were big and warm with rich colours and opulent furniture. Both of them had a king-sized bed and two singles. Both of the bathrooms were huge, and each had a jetted tub. Even the minibar was fully stocked with alcohol and snacks.

I'd forgotten what staying in places like this was like. Up until now, the accommodations had been more modest, which was fine with me. For the most part, they were nothing more than a place to sleep.

"This will pass over." Zeke stepped up behind me. He placed his hands on my shoulders and started to massage lightly.

I dropped my chin to my chest and sighed.

"Why is it always something? Just when I think we might be able to catch our breath, something else happens. When do we get a break?"

"Right now," he said firmly. "We can lock ourselves away in here and forget the rest of the world exists."

Asher moved to stand in front of me and took my hands in his. "Except when we open the door to people delivering food and alcohol."

"Except for then," Zeke agreed. "But someone else can open the door." He slid his hands from my shoulders, down my sides to my hips. "We can get busy in other ways."

"Yes we can," Asher agreed. He drew us both into the second room and Zeke closed the door behind us.

"Oh? Like what?" I asked teasingly. As if I didn't know exactly what was going on.

"Like this." Asher pulled me to him, tilted his head and pressed his mouth to mine. His stubble tickled my lips and chin, but I liked the way it felt.

I kissed him back, hungry not just to forget the world, but to be touched and to touch them. I pressed the tip of my tongue to his lips and inside his mouth when he opened it to me. He tasted like the cola he drank on the plane, with a hint of salt I guessed came from the tiny bag of peanuts. He'd complained they weren't big enough and ate them in a mouthful or two.

Zeke slipped his hands up the back of my shirt and unhooked my bra. The cups dropped, letting my breasts fall free under the fabric of my shirt.

The sudden rush of cool air made me shiver and my nipples hardened into points.

Zeke's arms snaked around me, rucking my shirt up past my navel. He cupped my breasts and rolled my nipples between his thumbs and forefingers.

My knees already wanted to give way at the hot heat that coursed through my body.

Asher's lips left mine and he started to nibble my neck and my throat.

"Abbie," he said softly. "I love you."

A flutter of butterflies did a dance around my stomach. Had I heard him right?

Without hesitation, I whispered back, "I love you too."

Asher pulled back and smiled at me, then over my shoulder. "Zeke, I love you."

Zeke leaned around me to kiss him. "I love you too, babe." He kissed me next. "I love you."

Even though we'd said it to each other before, this was the first time saying it in front of someone else. Of all people, Asher should be included in moments like this.

"I love you," I replied.

"Perfect." He gripped the hem of my shirt and pulled it up over my head. My bra quickly followed, along with the rest of my clothes.

And then all of theirs.

I would never get tired of seeing their bodies. Firm chests, rock hard abs, the Vs of their hips, broad shoulders, strong, veiny arms, big hands with long, thick fingers. They looked like gorgeous statues, with tattoos to add to the chiselled, perfect artistry.

And here I was, right in the middle. For the millionth time I wondered how I got so lucky.

Between both of these rock gods, they manoeuvred me over to the bed. They lay me down so I was stretched out, on my back, on Asher's firm chest and stomach.

Asher wound his arms around me to hold me in place and take his turn working my nipples.

Zeke bent my knees and placed each of my feet to the side of Asher's legs, opening me up to him. He propped himself on one elbow so he wasn't resting too much weight on Asher, and lowered his mouth down between my thighs.

His eyes on my face, Zeke started to lick at my pussy. Lightly at first, teasing with the tip of his tongue. Then faster and firmer, with ever-growing pressure and urgency, like he was starving for every drop of the juices he could get from me.

Asher's cock pressed into the side of my ass. I reached around behind me to curl my fingers around his thick, rock hard length. I was certain I could feel the blood throbbing through him with as much need as Zeke's mouth.

Zeke slowly slid a finger into me. Then another. "You're so wet," he said, his voice muffled by my pussy. "You're always so ready for us. Such a fucking goddess."

With six hot guys around to ruin my panties on an hourly basis, it was difficult to be anything but ready. As for goddess, I'd take that any day. Goddess and my six smokin' hot gods.

Hell yeah.

He worked me inside and out until I was ready to scream the whole hotel down. Between his tongue and the way Asher pinched and rolled my nipples, all I could do was shatter into a thousand rainbow shards and shudder and buck.

I bit my lip as wave after wave of firework-filled pleasure washed over me. Stars glittered in my vision. My hips moved, grinding my clit against Zeke's face, frantic to keep the high going for as long as I could.

I threw back my head and moaned and sobbed with how fucking good it felt. I wanted to stay right here in this place for eternity, but the tsunami crashed over, then slowly withdrew, leaving me to pant and whimper before the last drops left.

Like the gods, and gentlemen, they were, they let me catch my breath before Asher rolled us over and knelt between my legs.

Zeke moved up the bed and kissed me with his shining lips that tasted of me. Then he kissed Asher.

Asher traced his tongue all around Zeke's lips, then his own. "Yummy. I'd like to have the taste of both of you in my mouth. If you want to." He gave Zeke's cock a hungry glance, like he was looking at a juicy, perfectly done steak.

"I want to." Zeke scooted up a little further until his cock was a centimetre from Asher's nose and close to my face. "I want to a lot."

Far out, that was hot.

My body throbbed, heat pulsing in my core, when Asher eagerly opened his mouth and let Zeke slip his tip between his lips.

The sight, and wet smacking sound of Asher sucking, made me groan with renewed urgency.

"Asher, please," I begged. "I need you to fuck me." I wanted him inside me, yesterday.

His eyes flicked down to me and he nodded. His brow creased in concentration, Asher slid his cock into my wet but still very thirsty pussy.

Zeke and I let Asher set the pace of sucking and fucking. He slid his mouth off Zeke's cock and on again, as he slid out and back into me.

Zeke tangled his fingers in my hair while his other hand lightly cupped the back of Asher's head.

Zeke let out a guttural groan of pleasure. "You two are so *fucking* amazing." He punctuated his words with strokes into Asher's mouth.

"No, you," I said breathlessly. I reached over to ghost my fingers around Zeke's balls and the base of his cock. I ran my other hand over Asher's back, lightly raking my nails down and around his firm skin.

When Asher groaned, I dug them in firmer. If he wanted scratch marks, I was happy to oblige. The guys all wore them like a mark of honour when I did it. Like they'd fucked a wildcat and survived.

I was vaguely aware of the door opening and closing. The bed dipped as Penn sat down beside us.

"Is this a private party or can anyone join?" His gaze flicked over to the guys, then back to me. Judging by the heated look in his eyes, he liked what he saw. All of it.

"You're welcome to join in, sir," I said, a smile on my lips.

He eyed my mouth. "Cute that you really thought I was asking." He undid his jeans and slid them down his hips, freeing his erection. He lay on his side, his hips beside my face. "Suck my cock."

Aware that Zeke and Asher were watching with

wide eyes, I said, "Yes, sir," and opened my mouth to let him press his tip inside.

"Mmmm, yeah," Zeke groaned. "You guys are all amazing."

"Yes, we really fucking are," Penn agreed. He started to thrust slowly in and out of my mouth, his eyes half closed.

Asher and I both made sounds of agreement around our mouthfuls, and Asher started to pound into me harder and faster.

Two sets of wet sucking sounds, coupled with moans from Zeke and Penn, and the way Asher filled me with his thick length, drove me toward the wild, ragged edge of pleasure.

I came with a soft wash of orgasm, that whispered through me like sinking into a warm bath. It made my toes curl and my breath come in pants out my nose. A faint shudder passed through my core before it was gone. Barely a second later, another, more intense orgasm flooded through me. This one had me gasping, but it was the third that followed in its wake that had me crying out around Penn's heated flesh.

I saw stars a thousand universes over and drew an orgasm out of Asher at the same time. He rolled his hips, grinding into me, while at the same time choking on Zeke's cock. He must have clamped his mouth around the singer's dick, because Zeke swore and grunted as he too came.

Penn was last, but not far behind. He wound his fingers around a section of my hair and said, "Suck harder."

I couldn't have called him sir, or anything else, if I wanted to. My mouth was too busy and my mind was still coming down from the heights.

So I sucked harder.

"That's it," Penn said approvingly. "Good girl." He tugged my hair and slid in and out faster between my lips. "Take all of me, dirty girl." He thrust to the back of my throat again and again. "Fuck yeah."

He wound his fingers so tight into my hair it hurt, but the pain was exquisite, like Tully's paddle.

I sucked as hard as I could, as deep as I could, loving the sensation of him sliding in and out, the taste of him, the heat of his body. Blowing a guy, especially one I cared about, was hands down one of my favourite things to do. I could do it all day, happily. That and sing. Okay, and come. If I could do all three at once, I'd be a happy girl.

"I'm going to come in your mouth," Penn said. "You're going to take every drop of my cum down your throat and you're going to swallow it."

"Shit, that's hot," Asher said. Zeke must have slipped out of him, since he could talk again.

"It really is," Zeke agreed.

I wished I could see all of their faces, but the view of Penn's chiselled, rock hard stomach wasn't bad either.

Penn's fingers tightened and his hips rocked before convulsing as he came. As promised, a fountain of hot cum blossomed in my mouth. I held it while he milked himself for every last drop and ragged pant.

Finally he slid out of me and locked his eyes on my face.

I looked back at him and swallowed.

He smiled. "Good girl. You blew me like a dirty, obedient whore."

That made me feel warm all over. And aroused again.

## 18

ABBIE

"I REMEMBER before we got big, I always wanted to play at Wembley," Tully said. He stood behind me, his arms around me, head resting lightly on my shoulder.

"It is pretty much the holy grail of places to play," I said. "Literally, because a grail is actually a bowl, not a goblet."

The place was enormous. For the first time in a while, I was actually scared of the idea of stepping out there.

As usual, Blazing Violet had the audience hyped up into a frenzy, but would that last when I stepped out onto the stage?

"I know it's hard to keep the stresses of the last couple of days from getting to you," he said in my ear. "You're going to knock their socks off, just like every other night."

Thankfully he didn't tell me not to let it get to me, because I couldn't have kept that from happening if I tried. The press was still outside the hotel this morning when we left for the soundcheck. They were also outside the stadium when we arrived. Some of them shouted questions to the guys about the tour, so there was some hope they might move on from me sooner or later. Most, though, were directed at me.

"I keep thinking about Pete," I said. "We first assumed someone did something to him." That was an easy assumption, under the circumstances.

"Now—now, I don't know what to think. The police said it was an accident. Maybe they're right and that's all it was." They were the experts in these kinds of things, right? In theory anyway.

"And if it wasn't, was it the twins?" Tully asked.

"Right. What reason would they have for doing it? And why didn't we see them?" I twisted around to look at him.

"Do they need a reason? After what they did to Penn, I would think they're capable of just about anything, including that. In Pete's case, he was friends with my father."

I blinked. "And anyone who was friends with Xavier Lang—"

"Is an enemy of Reuben Brantley," Tully finished.

"So...not an accident," I concluded.

Shit.

"Potentially not," he agreed. "They might have also have thought they could score some points with Zeke by getting rid of someone who was stalking you."

"How sweet," I said sarcastically. "They're the last people on Earth I want romantic gestures from." After a moment, I added, "Except maybe Reuben. And every journalist that's been outside everywhere I've been for the last two days. And... Okay, the list might be longer than I thought." I sighed out my nose.

"They can leave the romantic gestures to us," Tully said.

I almost asked if he would kill someone for me, but I knew the answer. If that was something he had to do, then he would do it. I freaking hoped it will never come to that.

"I'm sorry, I didn't mean to be a downer," I said. "We should be enjoying this, not talking about all the stuff that's happened."

"You could never be a downer." He kissed my

cheek. "Sometimes you need to get things off your chest." He cupped one of my breasts and gave it a gentle squeeze.

Equally gently, I elbowed him in the chest. "Yes you do."

He chuckled. He took his hand off my breast to clap when Blazing Violet finished their last song.

I joined in the applause and added a whistle and a shout of appreciation. The guys all screamed and clapped almost as loud as the audience.

Violet and the guys waved their goodbyes and headed down off the stage.

I gave each a high-five as they passed, except Violet, whom I hugged.

"Knock 'em dead," she told me before she hurried off to have a shower.

"You're up," Zeke said with a grin.

That was the exact moment I froze.

I hadn't had stage fright since the first time I stepped out onto one, but I had it right now. More than a quiver of nerves, or a moment of second thought, my whole body shook. Sweat sprang out on my palms and under my arms.

I was glued to the spot with stone cold terror.

"Abbie?" Zeke frowned. "Are you okay?"

My voice trembled. "No. I am not o-fucking-kay.

I don't think I can do it."

I was vaguely aware of the audience stamping their feet and getting restless.

The guys were all in front of me then, looking at me with five almost identical expressions of worry.

The sixth—Penn, of course—rolled his eyes.

"Of course you can do it," Asher said. "Listen to the fans. They want you out there singing to them."

Macquarie and Jewel, who backed me up, were already out there on stage, waiting. Probably wondering what the fuck I was doing. Honestly, I was wondering too.

"Do they?" I asked. "What if they don't?"

The stadium didn't allow concertgoers to bring in anything they could use as a projectile, even if they could get close enough, but they could throw insults and jeers. I could step out there only to be booed back off. What if they thought I had something to do with Pete's death? Or any of the other deaths? Or what if they hated the fact I was with the guys at all? Or hated my music? Or the little black dress I was wearing that the guys all seemed to like? Or—

I tried to take a step forward, but my feet wouldn't move. I wanted to cry but I wasn't sure if it was fear, frustration or a combination of the two. If I didn't step out there tonight, I may never step out anywhere ever again.

But I couldn't move. My feet were paralysed with anxiety.

"For fuck's sake," Penn growled. Without another word, he grabbed my hand and yanked me towards the stairs.

I stumbled a couple of steps, but had no choice but to walk, or be dragged.

"I can't—" I started to say.

"You fucking can, and you fucking will," he said. "This is what you do."

He raised his arm as we stepped out on stage, hand in hand. He gave the audience a bow as if all of this was rehearsed.

I thought he would dump me at the front of the stage and shove a microphone in my hand. Instead, he led me over to his keyboard.

"Sit." He pointed to the stool.

I sat.

Jewel frowned at me from where she stood behind her keyboard. Penn wouldn't let anyone else play his. She looked confused.

I shrugged. I didn't know what the hell was going on either. Well, I kinda did, but Penn was unpredictable, so who knew how this might end?

He slipped in beside me and moved the microphone over so it was between us both.

He leaned over and whispered, "Breathe," in my ear. "You know this song. All you have to do is sing it."

My fear gave way to anger at being dragged out here like this. At some point, that might become gratitude, but right now I was pissed off at him. He could have at least given me another couple of minutes to get my shit together. I would have... eventually. Maybe.

Rationally, I knew I didn't have a couple of minutes. The audience was waiting. Right now, they were cheering. Probably for him, but I would take it.

He put his hands on the keys and started to play the beginning of "Lock Me In."

I looked at him in surprise. Of all the songs I thought he might play, this wasn't one of them. Given how personal it was to him, I never thought he'd want to share it with me. Not like this.

I leaned towards the microphone and started to sing.

"LOCKED BY REALITY,
*Caught up in the flow.*

*Shaken by the maelstrom,*
*Ripped to the bone."*

IN SPITE of how dark and intense the lyrics were, all of my fear melted away until I didn't even know why I had it in the first place. If anyone was shouting insults at me, I couldn't hear them. All I heard was ninety thousand people singing the words to Penn's song. Singing along to me.

Now I wasn't so pissed at Penn. Apparently he knew what I needed better than I did. A kick in the ass to get going. Singing with him didn't hurt either. Our voices blended so well together. Not as smoothly and practised as Zeke and I, but this was a rock concert. It didn't matter if we were a little rough around the edges. If anything, it was better that we were. If people wanted smooth and polished, they would go and see an orchestra play. If they wanted gritty and rough as fuck, they would come to us.

We finished singing and Penn sat back, a satisfied look on his gorgeous face.

Normally, I'd be tempted to punch him for looking so smug, but this time it was justified.

"There, now you won't steal my solo," he said.

He grunted as I elbowed him in the stomach. "Now get the fuck on your feet and sing, woman." He leaned in to speak right into my ear. "Enjoy standing up while you can, because after this I expect you to spend a lot of time on your knees."

I turned my head so I could talk in his ear. "Promises promises, sir."

"You can bet it's a fucking promise." He stood and helped me to my feet before he gave the audience a bow.

"I'm sure it is," I told him. "Now get the fuck off my stage." I waved him away.

I knew he hadn't done this so I would blow him off until my mouth hurt, but I might do that for him after this anyway.

I mean, we'd both enjoy it. Win-win.

He gave me a look like he wasn't sure if he should kiss me or fuck me in front of ninety thousand people. Since neither of those options was a good idea, and he knew it, he grinned and started towards the back of the stage.

Before he left, he couldn't help himself. He stopped, turned back around and gave the crowd another bow. The smartass even blew them a kiss.

He must have spent a lot of time watching Zeke; the lead singer was starting to rub off on him.

The crowd screamed and cheered as he headed offstage. He was certainly popular with audiences. And didn't he know it?

I grabbed a microphone out of one of the stands and brought it to my mouth. "Beau Pennington, ladies and gentlemen. He is shy, isn't he?"

I looked over my shoulder to see him roll his eyes before he disappeared from view.

I let the cheers die down, before I spoke again. "Some of you might know me. For those who don't, my name is Abbie Hart. I have a confession to make."

The crowd fell into an uneasy silence. As silent as ninety thousand people could be. Yeah, they'd heard of me all right. I had a feeling they were expecting me to say something horrible.

I raised the microphone again. "The truth is, London is one of my favourite places on the planet. No one else goes wild like you guys."

Of course, that was the cue to go wild. And they did.

I nodded to the Jewel and Macquarie. They nodded back. They were professionals. This probably wasn't the weirdest thing they'd ever seen by any stretch of the imagination. I bet they had some stories to tell. I'd have to ask them sometime.

In the middle of all the cheering, I started to sing.

# 19

## ABBIE

I POKED Penn in the chest with my fingernail.

"If you ever drag me like that again, I'm going to rip off your balls and shove them down your throat." I poked him again but I was trying not to smile.

He stepped back through the door to our hotel rooms, grabbed my hands and pulled me toward him so my face almost bumped into his chin. "You talk a big game for a woman who was about to wet her panties." He leaned in and added, "I don't mean in a good way."

"I was not," I protested. I took a side step out of the way so Landon could close and lock the door behind us all.

"Were too," Penn said. "There's nothing wrong

with admitting you were shit scared. It happens to the best of us."

"It happens to you?" I asked, an eyebrow arched in question.

The corners of his mouth tugged upward in a slight smile. "Shit no, but thanks for admitting I'm the best of us."

I tried to poke him again but he held my wrists too tight. "You are such a smartass."

He smiled a little more. "And smart, too. I'm starting to think you don't hate me after all." He caught my lips with his in a rough kiss.

"I still do," I said against his mouth. "Very much."

I didn't hate him. I never had, even when he was an enormous dickhead just after we met. He was being territorial. Considering all the things I learnt about the guys since then, I understood why. Surrounded by violence and death, it was easier to keep new people away. Safer for them and for you.

"Back at you," he said. His hands still on my wrists, he pulled away and looked down at me. "I made you a promise out there on the stage. I intend to keep it."

My heart raced. If my panties weren't wet before, they were now. In a good way.

"What promise was that?" I asked innocently.

Apparently not caring the guys were arrayed around the room, sitting on chairs and beds, he said, "The one where I said you'd be on your knees."

"Oh, *that* one." I nodded slowly, as though it slipped my mind.

*Hell yeah, yes please.*

"Yeah, that," he growled playfully. "Do it. Get on your knees." He pushed me downwards by my wrists.

Aware every eye in the room was on me, I knelt. "Yes, sir."

More than one of the guys groaned.

Slowly, I undid the front of Penn's jeans and drew down the zip. I pushed his pants down his hips and freed his erection. As I curled my fingers around his hot, thick length, I became aware of most of the guys slipping into the other room. Only Tully stayed.

I worked Penn with my hand, making him stiffer. I glanced up at him. Usually, I hated being told what to do, but when he did it, it was hot as hell.

"Suck my cock," he ordered, his tone bordering on a moan.

"Yes, sir." I lowered my mouth to him, but instead of licking and teasing like I usually did, I took in as much of him as I could and clamped my lips around him like a vise.

I drew back oh, so slowly, sliding my mouth all the way down to his tip, then back up again.

He muttered something incoherent, but it sounded as though he liked it.

Encouraged, I kept doing that, slowly at first, then gradually quicker.

He tangled his fingers in my hair, tugging lightly every few moments.

In the corner of my eye, I saw Tully approach. He was deliciously naked, slowly running his hand up and down his own cock. The piercing in his tip glittered in the light of a lamp in the corner.

"Suck Tully," Penn ordered.

With a wet smacking sound, I took my lips off Penn and turned my face to take Tully into my mouth.

While I sucked him, Penn stripped off. In a matter of moments, I was on my knees in front of two gorgeous, tattooed rock gods.

A girl could get used to this.

I alternated sucking one guy for a few moments, then the other. My hands ran up and down their lengths and massaged their balls while I went back and forth.

"I need to be inside you," Penn said finally. His

fingers still curled in my hair, he encouraged me to stand up. "Put your hands up above your head."

I looked at him funny but did what he said.

He and Tully exchanged a glance before they both grabbed the hem of my dress and pulled it up over my head and off. Tully unhooked my bra and slid it down my arms while Penn pulled down my panties. I stepped out of them and let Penn lead me over to the bed.

"Kneel on the edge," he said. "On all fours."

I knelt.

Tully knelt in front of me, his body angled so I could take his cock back in my mouth.

Penn ran his hands over my ass, then leaned in to run his tongue from my clit to my rear hole.

I shivered deliciously.

He did that a few more times, then focused all of his attention on licking my clit and sliding his fingers inside me.

He brought me to the edge so quickly, I decided he knew how to play me better than any musical instrument. So well, it was almost not fair. I wasn't ready to come yet. At the same time, I didn't think I could stop myself.

Penn straightened up and leaned over me so his

chest was curled over my back, but with none of his weight on me.

"You're so wet and so close, but you're going to wait," he said.

I responded with a noise of frustration muffled by Tully's cock. I looked up at Tully as though he might save me from the frustration, but he just smiled and went on watching me work him with my mouth. I could almost see him taking note of what I liked. He was all about people enjoying the sensations life has to offer.

"I could get a paddle," Tully said helpfully.

*Shit. Yes please.*

"Get it," Penn growled.

Tully slipped his cock out of my mouth and stepped away for a minute or two. He came back with the black leather paddle he'd used on me before. He offered it to Penn, who grabbed it and started to run it lightly in circles around my ass cheeks.

Just when I thought that was all he would do, he raised the paddle and slapped me lightly, only hard enough for the slightest sting. The sections of leather cracked together.

That was nearly enough to make me come, even without being touched anywhere else.

Tully put a couple of fingers under my chin to tip it back. "You like that, don't you?"

"I like it harder," I said.

"What's the magic word?" Penn asked.

"Please, sir," I said.

He brought the paddle down harder. This time the sting was sharper, more intense.

I gasped out loud. "Ohhh, yeah. Like that." After a moment I added, "Sir."

"Good girl," Penn said. He paddled me a few more times while Tully slid his cock back into my mouth. As the pain almost became too much, Penn tossed the paddle aside, gripped my hips and positioned his cock at the entrance to my pussy.

The feeling of him sliding into my body made me moan. He felt so good. Just as good as it felt to have Tully fuck my mouth.

Both of them got into a rhythm of firm, even strokes into my body. The world disappeared in a haze of wet thrusts and sucks. I could happily stay right here in this place forever.

Right before I thought he might come, Tully pulled out and moved to sit beside me on the edge of the bed. He kissed my mouth and let his hands wander down across my breasts, over my nipples and down to my clit.

I moaned the moment he slid his fingers across my folds. I bucked against his hand, desperate to find my orgasm.

"Don't let her come until I say so," Penn said. He leaned over me and grazed my back with his teeth. "Do you hear me? No coming until I tell you to."

I managed to grind out the words, "Yes, sir."

As if that was his cue, Tully started working me even harder.

I decided they were both cruel assholes. Lucky for them I cared about both of them a lot, otherwise, I might come to spite them.

I gritted my teeth with the effort of staying on the edge and not going over. That was hard with Penn pounding into me, and Tully's fingers expertly teasing my clit. Not to mention the fact I kept picturing Penn's cock bumping into Tully's hand every now and again. I knew they weren't into each other like that, but the mental image still did it for me.

Penn's thrusts became faster and more frantic. "Not yet."

I wasn't sure if he was talking to me or himself. Maybe both.

He grunted and his fingers dug into my hips. I

rocked back into him, wanting to help him, so he would let me do the same.

"Not yet," Penn said again. His breathing was a ragged pant, to match mine. "Okay," Penn said finally. "You can let her come."

Like he flipped a switch, I was enveloped in an orgasm so intense I threw my head back and almost screamed at the ceiling. Somewhere in the back of my pleasure-flooded consciousness, I was aware of Penn coming too. Our moans and grunts were in sync like a symphony.

I left my body for approximately seven minutes. All I knew was where our bodies were all joined, and the ecstasy of an orgasm full of pink, purple and blue flashing lights. When I finally came down, I was gasping for breath and my head was feeling light.

"Lie back." Penn slid his now slick cock out of my body.

For a moment I thought he was talking to me, until Tully lay back and Penn guided me to straddle his hips. His hands on my sides, fingers almost touching my breasts, he lowered me onto Tully's cock.

"Ride him," Penn said.

"Yes, sir." I smiled down at Tully, who didn't seem to mind having the keyboardist boss us around.

Tully smiled back and gripped my hips to help me get a rhythm, sliding up and down his length.

Penn rolled one of my nipples between his thumb and forefinger while reaching down to rub my clit with his other hand. "You're going to come again."

I moaned. The way they were both touching me, I certainly was.

"What do you say?" Penn rubbed a little harder.

"Yes, sir." I glanced down where our bodies joined and saw Tully's cock slide past Penn's hand.

Holy shit.

I arched my back and rode Tully harder, until his breathing was a series of rapid gasps. I was already close to coming again.

"Not until I say so," Penn said, leaning over my shoulder so he could look me in the face.

I hissed at him playfully.

He chuckled and worked me harder. Asshole.

Tully groaned and thrust up into me harder and faster.

"Almost," Penn said. "Not yet."

I moaned.

"Okay, now," Penn said.

However he did it, I didn't care. Tully and I both came in unison, our bodies grinding together, slick with sweat and friction. I cried out louder this time, my voice mingling with Tully's moans and grunts.

"Fuck yeah," Tully ground out.

This time, my orgasm lasted longer, cresting several times until my whole body started to ache. Blood raced through every centimetre of me, taking tingles with it. My vision blurred. My heart pounded like a kick drum, louder in my ears than any concert I'd ever been to, or performed in. The pleasure reached a crescendo before finally starting to die away, like the last notes still echoing through a venue.

Exhausted, I slumped down over Tully until I caught my breath.

Penn flopped down beside us and we all lay there panting, satisfied.

For now.

# 20

ABBIE

"Happy release day." Asher dropped into the seat beside me. Zeke sat on the other side. That was how it was when we went anywhere these days. They were on either side of me, or one was in front and the other behind. No one from the press, or anyone else for that matter, could get close to me except the other guys.

"Thanks." I clicked my seatbelt and pulled out my phone. "Do you think we'll slip away unnoticed?"

They both laughed.

After a moment, I joined in. No one would fail to notice a huge, double-decker bus with the words *Wolf Venom* down the side in huge letters. It was definitely not subtle, by anyone's standards.

"The windows are tinted," Zeke said. "They can try to look in as much as they want, but they won't see anything." He nodded towards my phone. "Well?"

"I'm too scared to look," I admitted. I nodded to Jackson as he climbed on board the bus and sat up in the front near the driver. If he knew anything, he wasn't saying. That made me more nervous.

"You have nothing to be scared about," Asher said. "Everyone is going to love it. They'll be excited for your whole album to drop."

"Possibly." Or they would hate it and the label would drop me like a hot, greasy spring roll. The kind that had too much cabbage and not enough of whatever it was that went into greasy spring rolls. Yeah okay, that wasn't the best analogy, but close enough.

The rest of the album wouldn't be out until after the tour was over. This song was a teaser. An announcement, of sorts, that I had a new label and wasn't beaten out of the industry yet.

"If you don't look, then I'll look for you," Asher said. He made a grab for my phone but I pulled it out of his reach.

"Fine, I'll look." I turned on my screen and did a quick search for my name and a review.

The first one I found, I read out loud. *"Abbie Hart's new single, 'Inside Out', is a reminder of her unique talent. Ms Hart is currently on tour with Wolf Venom. Rumours suggest she is romantically involved with at least one member of the famous band. That certainly won't hurt her future career."*

I snorted. "So apparently I'm fucking my way to the top. At least they liked the song."

Shit like this didn't worry me. It was standard for the last…ever. Since I started singing. My sex life always seemed to be more important or interesting than my music. This particular reviewer could have said a lot worse than they had.

"Of course they did," Asher said. "It's awesome. And the drumming and guitar on it aren't bad either."

"You and Tully playing on it are what made it so good," I said.

"That's bullshit and you know it," Penn said from the other side of the bus. "It's good in spite of them." He looked like he was trying not to smile. If he wasn't careful, he might actually do it at some point. He might even get used to doing it.

Tully and Asher both flipped him off.

"It's good because you're all awesome," Landon

said. "Next time, I'm playing on your stuff too. We could be your backing band."

"Fuck that," Penn said. "We're nobody's backing band." After a moment he added, "That doesn't mean we can't help out if we have time."

"We'll make time," Channing said. "Jackson can always shuffle things around for us if he has to. Levi won't mind." Levi might, but it didn't sound like Channing was going to give him a choice.

I smiled appreciatively and tried not to look too surprised that Penn would make that offer. I was hoping he would, but it was always hard to tell with Penn. He'd probably want me to call him *sir* the entire time. Was it wrong that the thought made me tingly all over?

I clicked on the next review, and the one after that. Both made a brief, positive mention of the song, then either my supposed love life, or my alleged stalker and the string of deaths that followed me.

One went so far as to suggest the guys should be careful around me, even though Pete was dead. Evidently they thought I was bad luck. Even if I tried to tell the guys to stay away from me, they probably wouldn't.

What was I thinking? Of course they wouldn't.

They certainly weren't going to listen to some random person on the internet.

"Social media likes the song," Tully said, his eyes on his own phone. "It's number two on that video making app. There's a ton of videos on here already of people dancing to it, and..." He frowned at his screen. "I'm surprised they let that much nudity on there."

Asher leaned over for a look. "Yeah, that's...probably gonna get taken down really soon. Shame, he's got some moves. Although, if he keeps dancing like that, he's going to end up with bruises on his thighs."

"I don't think I want to see," I said. If it was one of the guys slapping his cock on his thighs, I would happily watch. But not some stranger.

"He's cute," Asher said. "But not as cute as you and Zeke. And the rest of you," he added, clearly knowing the rest of the guys would say something if he didn't.

"Don't you forget it," Penn said.

"I wouldn't because you won't let me," Asher said.

"True," Penn said unashamedly.

The tour bus slid out of the hotel gates, past a smaller contingent of press than the one that was there two days ago. They took photos of the bus and watched it pass by.

That was their cue to get on with their lives. Those that wouldn't be following us to Cardiff anyway. With any luck, the Welsh press had better things to do than chase us around.

Or chase me around at least. If they wanted to report on the tour, we would all be down for that. It wasn't every day that a group of hot, Australian rock gods toured the country.

Even though they couldn't see me, I couldn't resist flipping them off before we were out of sight. Hopefully they would sense it. Okay, it was as petty as hell, but it made me feel better. I felt better still knowing they couldn't see it. They gave me enough grief without photographing me doing that.

The guys could get away with it, apparently, but I couldn't.

I turned back to my phone and read a few more reviews. Most were favourable, some weren't. One described it as nothing more than marshmallow for the ears, that will only appeal to people under the age of six.

Whatever, I couldn't please everyone. My style of music wasn't everyone's jam. I didn't mind that. I certainly didn't mind appealing to children. If they stuck with me for the next twenty or thirty years, I'd be set.

What I did mind was when critics got personal with their criticism, like the one who couldn't resist mentioning my weight, and suggesting I should eat fewer burgers. It's the same old story—it's easy to say nasty things when you're hiding behind a keyboard.

Realistically, some of these people would say the same things to my face. Oh well, they were the ones who had to sleep with their negativity at night.

I'm not going to claim I wouldn't dwell on it, because I always did. The bad stuff always stuck in my brain stronger than the good stuff.

It's true what they say about people being their own worst enemy. I shouldn't be reading reviews in the first place. They weren't for me, they were for people to decide if they wanted to listen or not.

Personally, I never paid any attention to reviews of other people's work. I listened and if I liked it, I listened again. If I didn't like it, then I didn't. Simple.

Why would anyone make up their minds based on a review anyway? It wasn't a three-hour movie. It was a three-minute song.

Asher started drumming on the seat beside him with his fingers.

I glanced over to see him looking out the window, obviously unaware of what he was doing. And the fact I was staring at him. He was so fucking gorgeous I could hardly believe I was on the same bus with him or the rest of the guys. How did an ordinary girl from the suburbs end up here? Was Tully right about it being fate, or some design by the universe? I couldn't think up a better explanation than that. Except luck, and I'd never been a big believer in luck, good or bad. We did shit and that shit had consequences. Sometimes bad, sometimes awesome, like this.

"Are we playing guess that song?" Zeke asked, breaking through my thoughts.

I turned to see him smiling past me to Asher.

Asher looked over at him and grinned. He was even more gorgeous when he did that. So much so, my heart did a little leap. How could I not be head over heels for these guys?

"We could," Asher said. He started to tap more intentionally.

"The Wheels on the Bus?" Landon suggested jokingly.

"Hot Cross Buns?" Channing grinned. "Or Mary Had a Little Lamb."

"Baby Shark," Penn said with a smirk. He clearly knew just saying those words would make the tune stick in our minds.

"No. No. And hell no," Asher said. "Don't you guys know any adult songs?"

"Like Fuck Your Face?" Zeke asked.

Asher frowned. "Is that an actual song?"

Zeke snorted a laugh. "I'd be surprised if it wasn't. If someone can put it in a song, they will." It wasn't the kind of thing Wolf Venom would get away with, but if they could, they'd try.

"True." Asher nodded. "Anyway, that wasn't the song. I thought you guys would be better at this than that."

"We know the song," Penn said. "But giving you shit is more fun than playing this game."

Asher stuck his tongue out at him. "Can we throw Penn off the bus yet?"

"Not while it's moving," Zeke said.

Asher craned his neck to look towards the front of the bus.

"What are you doing?" I asked.

"Looking for a traffic light." Asher smiled and wiggled his brows. "We have to hit a red one sooner or later."

"I vote we throw Asher off the bus while it *is* moving," Penn said. "But not yet. Let's wait to get out on the motorway and the bus is going a fuck ton faster."

"No one is throwing anyone off the bus," Jackson called out.

"Spoilsport," Asher said.

Jackson turned around in his seat. "Yep. That's part of my job description. You didn't know that?"

"I suspected it," Asher said. "You're always trying to stop us from having a good time."

"Maybe we *should* throw Asher off the bus," Jackson mused.

Asher laughed. "I know you love me."

"If you say so." Jackson turned around the other way.

"He just hides it well," Asher said.

"Very well," Penn agreed. "So well we'd—" He froze mid-word.

"What is it?" Zeke asked. "Penn?"

Penn was staring straight ahead at Jackson, who had turned back around in his chair and was staring at Penn.

Jackson had his phone in his hand and his face was pale. He undid his seatbelt and slowly walked through the bus towards us. "What is this?" he demanded.

"What is what?" Zeke asked evenly. "Whatever it is, I'm sure there's a logical explanation for it." He looked as confused and worried as I felt.

Jackson turned his phone around to show a photo of Penn in the park in Mumbai. It was taken from a distance, but he was clearly trying to climb the railing. Zeke, Asher and I were on the left side of the screen.

"What the fuck were you doing?" Jackson asked.

## 21

### PENN

"Fuck." I looked at myself on the screen.

It was obvious exactly what was going on. I knew it. Jackson knew it. We all knew it.

Jackson's expression was a combination of disappointment and frustration.

I thought about making up some kind of bullshit story, but there was no point. I was screwed.

"I was as high as fuck," I admitted. "I thought I could fly. They thought otherwise." I jerked my head towards Zeke, Asher and Abbie. "I didn't do it to myself. I had some unwanted help."

I didn't expect Jackson to believe me. Why would he? I'd screwed up enough in the past, he had little reason to trust me. Especially when it came to drugs.

"I know," Jackson said.

I frowned. "Huh?" What the hell? "What do you mean, you know?"

He swiped across the screen to the previous photo. It was one of me being held by the arm by twin pricks. My mouth was twisted into a snarl, but they looked amused. Assholes.

"None of you looked surprised," Jackson said slowly, with barely controlled anger. "Apparently I'm the only one in the dark about one of my guys getting assaulted." He shook his head and grimaced. "Why did I have to learn about this from a friend of a friend who works for Mumbai police? Lucky for you, they wiped these photos after they sent me copies."

"Thank fuck for that," I muttered.

"Yeah, thank fuck for that," he said sarcastically. He crouched down and grabbed the corner of the seat. "Did it slip your mind to mention this?"

I answered his question with one of my own. "Is my contract terminated?"

If that was the case, they wouldn't have to throw me off the bus. I might just as well jump.

"His contract clearly states no drugs," Zeke said. He looked worried and pissed off.

Jackson rounded on him. "Do you want me to tell Levi to terminate his contract?"

"Shit no," Zeke said. "We didn't tell you because —"

Jackson waved him off and turned back to me. "Do you think I'm not capable of exercising a bit of discretion?"

"Zeke is right," I said. I felt my career trickling down the toilet at the back of the bus. "My contract is clear." I was totally and completely screwed. If I saw those twin assholes again, I was going to rip both their heads off.

"Your contract states that if you do drugs it will be terminated," Jackson agreed. He swiped back to the photo of me climbing the railing. "Was any of this voluntary?" He looked like he was desperate for me to say it wasn't.

"Fuck no," I said firmly. "It was one hundred percent not consensual." I pinched the bridge of my nose. "I've worked hard to stay clean, you know that. I wanted to keep it that way. I don't know if they were targeting me or just any one of us." I shrugged and sighed. "I was in the wrong place at the wrong time."

"That's why no one is going anywhere by themselves from now on," Zeke said, his tone rock solid.

He eyed Channing, who still looked unapologetic after going off by himself in the airport.

Jackson adjusted his position on the floor. "So you didn't tell me because you thought you'd be out on your rear immediately."

"Yeah," I said. "It's a pretty wild story when you think about it. People usually get shit slipped into their drinks, not their veins." I frowned. "Wait, were those photos from Pete's phone?"

"Yeah, they were," Jackson said. "Seems it wasn't just Abbie he was following. Lucky for you he took both photos."

"Because you wouldn't have believed me if you hadn't seen me with those assholes?" I asked.

Jackson shrugged. "Like you said, it's a wild story. I am going to have to explain all of this to Levi. If Pete took photos, then chances are someone else did. I need to deal with this before it becomes a problem. But for fuck's sake, the next time something like this happens, tell me. I can't help you if I don't know about it."

"Yeah." I felt like a kid who got told off by his parents for riding his bike too fast down the street. Luckily they only caught me once and it was totally worth it. Considering how steep the street was, it was a miracle I didn't fall off and break any bones.

What can I say? I've always been a live fast kind of guy.

"After everything we've been through, you really think you can't trust me?" Jackson asked. He looked hurt. "How many times in the last few weeks in particular have I helped you all to clean up messes?"

"We appreciate it," Zeke said. "You're right, we should have told you. We just…"

"Don't think of me as one of you?" Jackson finished for him. "I might not be in the band, but I think we can all agree I have a vested interest in everything you do. As much as all of you." He looked around at each of us, one after the other. "I'm not going to throw any of you under, or off, the bus." He managed a faint smile.

"We know," Zeke said. "We also know there are things you'd prefer not to get involved in. If it wasn't for that photo with the twins in it, what would you do? You'd have to decide between talking to Levi and covering for us."

"Or taking my word for what happened," I suggested.

"That too," Zeke said with a nod. "We didn't want to put you in that position if we could avoid it. You do a shit load for us as it is. Above and beyond. I don't think lying to Levi is in your job description, is it?"

"No, and I'd prefer not to do it," Jackson agreed. "If no other photos surfaced, then I wouldn't have to. I just…wouldn't tell him."

"I'm pretty sure that's still considered lying," Asher remarked.

Jackson shrugged. "I consider it as what he doesn't know doesn't hurt him. Fortunately, I don't have to do that in this instance. I'll tell him every-thing and he'll understand."

"How many things have you not told us so you don't hurt us?" Asher asked.

"That's a good question, Ash," I said. I gave Jackson a sceptical look.

"Thank you, Penny," Asher said. "I thought so too."

We both gave Jackson a sceptical look.

Jackson rose. "I'm going to plead manager's privi-lege on this one. Just like there are many things you haven't told me. We don't have to know everything about each other."

"We don't?" Asher asked. "I thought we did. I mean, we pretty much do, don't we?"

"Most things," Tully agreed. "We spend a lot of time together. Sometimes there's nothing else to do but talk about ourselves."

"Usually I just listen to the other guys talk about themselves," I said.

"That's true," Asher said. "Hey, Jackson, are you and Levi sleeping together?"

The question caught all of us off guard, Jackson most of all. His face turned slightly pink.

"None of your business," he muttered.

"You know who most of us are sleeping with," Asher protested.

"Which is none of *my* business," Jackson said. He shoved his phone in his pocket and hurried back to sit down at the front of the bus.

"I'd say that's a yes," Landon said. He was sitting sideways in his seat with his legs draped over Channing's lap.

"Sounds like a yes to me," Channing agreed.

"Me too," Abbie said. She shot Jackson an apologetic look when he glanced over his shoulder at her. "I just want everyone to be happy."

Jackson shook his head and turned away.

"At least we now know what to say when we want to distract him from yelling at us," I pointed out. Honestly, I was as relieved as fuck Jackson believed the truth. And that creepy Pete took the first photo, and didn't delete it off his phone. This whole conversation would be different if he had. Ugh, great, I got to be grateful to a creepy-ass stalker asshole. It was better than flying home in disgrace and the rest of the guys hating me forever.

And me hating myself forever.

"I wonder what else he took photos of," I mused. Probably all sorts of inappropriate shit. I was sure his family were sad he was dead, but I couldn't say the same. He seemed like one fucked up dude.

Okay, that was hypocritical of me, because so was I, but I didn't take photos of people without their knowledge or consent. I didn't stalk anyone. I didn't murder anyone. Maybe I wasn't such a bad guy after all.

Nah, yes I was. I was okay with that.

"I'm more concerned that anyone else took photos," Zeke said. "If those leak, we're going to be right in the middle of another shit storm." He ran a hand over the back of his head and exhaled deeply.

I shrugged. "Nothing I can't deal with. And if they get busy hassling me, they might leave Abbie alone for a while." I was perfectly capable of telling pushy tabloid assholes to fuck off.

"I'd like that," she said. After a moment, her face turned red and she added, "I mean, I hope they leave me alone. I don't want them to hassle you, or anyone else."

I knew that was what she meant, but I couldn't resist giving her shit about it.

"Sure. You could have a good laugh over the things they say about me online. Why not? I've had a good laugh about stuff they say about you." I gave her the slightest twitch of my eyebrows.

She snorted. "You're so full of shit. Do you even read the stuff they write about me online?"

She had me there. "Nah. I prefer to read about actual celebrities. You know, like the ones who are famous for being on reality TV shows. Rich people behaving badly are more entertaining than you are."

"The irony," Zeke said.

I turned to him and frowned. "Are you suggesting I'm a rich person behaving badly?"

Zeke grinned. "If the hat fits."

I sneered at him. He wasn't wrong though. That description fit me pretty well, especially the part about being rich.

Abbie laughed. "I think you just got called out, Penn."

"I'm a *big* boy," I said. "I can handle it." Before Asher made any remarks about me handling myself,

I said, "Almost as well as Abbie can handle me. Right, Tully?"

Sharing with the lead guitarist was a little weird at first, but it worked. Instead of just getting to boss Abbie around, I got to boss both of them around. Plus it was just the right combination of watching and taking part.

I fully intend to do it again. Often.

"Abbie is very good at handling all of us," Tully agreed. "I'm not even trying to get the image of her red ass out of my mind."

Yeah, paddling her was one of my favourite bits. That and…all the rest of it.

I might have to get myself a paddle so I didn't have to borrow one from Tully. I surprised myself by how much I liked using it. Then again, I always liked it a bit rough. Thankfully, she seemed to enjoy it too. From what I saw, she enjoyed everything all of us guys had thrown at her so far.

I was curious as to what she would do with Landon and Channing and when. All three of them seemed to be taking their time, knowing it would happen when they were ready.

Whatever. The longer it took, the more time I had with Abbie. A part of me wondered if it should feel weird to share a woman with five other guys, but we shared everything else. Why not a woman? Especially one who seemed turned on by the lightest touch. I loved that she wasn't afraid of her sexuality or that of the rest of us. She just slotted in like another piece of our crazy puzzle.

The best piece.

## 22

ABBIE

"BRITISH PUBS ARE THE BEST." Asher lowered a tray of fresh pints of beer to the centre of the table, and handed me my vodka and lemon.

I nodded my thanks and tried to smile around a mouthful of chicken schnitzel. There was enough food on my plate for about three of me. If I ate like this every day, there would quickly be three times as much of me. In spite of that, I was still eying the dessert menu.

"Are you knocking Australian pubs?" Zeke asked.

"No, but if I'm not careful I'm going to knock my head." Asher looked up to the low ceiling above us. Low compared to how tall he and the other guys were.

A hundred years ago, when the pub was built,

people were my height, so it suited me just fine. Sometimes it paid to be short. Or petite, as I preferred to describe myself.

The tour bus driver managed to find us a pub in a small town somewhere in Wales.

I couldn't remember the place name and stood no chance of pronouncing it. It was the kind of town where most people didn't know who any of us were, so apart from a couple of stares, we were left alone. It was exactly what we needed after a hectic few weeks and a buttload of unwanted attention.

"You'll only do it once, then you'll learn how to duck," Zeke told him teasingly. He leaned over to give Asher a kiss. Then the other way to give me one.

"I'll learn or I'll knock myself out cold," Asher said. "Either way, you're right, I'll only do it once."

"Don't knock yourself out cold," Jackson said. "We need you conscious for tomorrow night's concert."

"I'm sure Kyle would fill in for him," I teased. I ducked my head over to the table where some of the tour staff sat.

Kyle raised his glass in a toast of agreement. He was one of those guys who had a lot of experience playing and working on different tours and albums, but always had half an eye out for a more permanent gig with a band. Hooking up with an established act would be easier than starting from scratch with a new one.

"Back off, Kyle," Asher said in mock warning. He held up his fists as though he was going to fight the other guy for the privilege.

"Let's not have a drummer-off," Jackson said dryly.

"I'd win," Danny said from where he sat with Violet and the rest of their band.

"Hey, Abbie," Violet called out. "Can't you just imagine them all comparing cock sizes?"

I laughed. "I totally can." As long as they didn't ask me to judge. Whoever won that would have the biggest head in the room. Both kinds of head.

"There's no need for that," Penn said.

"There isn't?" I asked. For a moment, I thought he was going to say something sensible like size didn't matter. I should have known better.

"No," he said. "I'd win." He looked smug.

Considering they'd all seen each other naked, they had a fair idea of who had what if they'd cared to look.

"Keep telling yourself that," Landon said. For once, he was sitting on the other side of me.

Apparently, since I was sitting with my back to

the wall, Asher and Zeke deemed it safe enough to let me sit beside someone else. It was a nice change.

Channing leaned forward to see around Landon and asked me, "Do women compare breast sizes?"

"Sometimes," I said. "Especially when they start getting them. Some develop earlier than others. Some take a while but catch up big time."

I certainly had. I stopped growing up at about the same time my chest started growing out. Lucky for me, I ended up with decent sized breasts but not too huge. Enough for a handful in each hand.

"And some never catch up," Penn said.

Asher patted him on the shoulder. "It's okay. You could always have implants."

"Fuck off," Penn told him. "If anyone needs implants, it's you. Ball implants."

"Ouch," Asher winced. "Why are you coming at me like that? For the record, there's nothing wrong with my balls. They're exactly what I need them to be. Right Abbie?"

"Right," I agreed. "There is also nothing wrong with people needing, or wanting breast implants. Whatever makes people happy and comfortable with themselves."

"I'll drink to that," Tully said. He raised his glass.

We all followed suit, meeting in the middle to clink. We even avoided breaking any glasses. Go us.

We finished eating dinner and the publican came to clear away our plates.

"We have a local band playing tonight," he said in his lovely Welsh lilt. He'd introduced himself as Alan when we first arrived. "Nothing of your calibre, of course, but I hope you will enjoy what you hear. They go by the name of Fandango Flit."

"I'm sure they'll be amazing." I hoped they didn't want us to get up and sing or play. I was pretty sure Alan was one of the few people who knew who we were. Personally, I would prefer to keep it that way.

The band set up in the corner of the room. They consisted of three men; one singing, one playing guitar and the other on drums. They had a basic set up, but when they started to play, they were pretty good. Perfect for a little Welsh pub and a relaxing night. Like most pub bands, they started out with popular songs we all knew. Before too long, people got up to dance.

"Would you like to dance with me?" Landon asked when they played a slow song.

"I'd love to," I said.

When he offered me his hand, I took it.

We stepped over to the makeshift dance floor,

which was just an area where tables had been cleared after dinner was finished. Landon slipped his arms around my waist and I put mine around his neck. We didn't so much dance as sway to the music.

"This is the most normal night I've had since..." I had to stop and think about it. "Since Zeke and I met."

At least, the hour or so before we had a gun pulled on us was normal. If you can call giving a blowjob to a complete stranger under a table in a nightclub normal.

I often wondered if I'd have done it if I knew who he was at the time. I doubted it. I would have been too scared of fucking up with Wolf Venom for it to have occurred to me.

"It's been a while for me too," Landon agreed. "Like, before the band got big. I used to go down to the pub on Friday and Saturday night and hang out with friends, just like this. Then I met Channing and the other guys and it's hard to go anywhere without being stared at. I think I forgot what it feels like. Kinda makes me wonder if all the fame is worth it."

"I can totally relate to that," I said. "I remember the days when I could go clothes shopping without being stared at." Granted, I did most of my shopping online, but I liked to try things on when I had the chance. And have coffee with my friends. Back when I had friends to have coffee with.

"I'm surprised you could do anything without being stared at," he said. "Even without being famous. You're beautiful." His hands slipped down so he cupped my ass while we swayed.

"So are you," I said. "Having blue hair makes you stand out a bit too." Just a *tiny* bit.

He grinned. "That's the point. I've always liked to be different. Not like a face full of tattoos different, but I've tried a lot of hair colours and I'm always thinking about new places to get pierced. Like maybe Jacob's ladder for my cock. Channing has a Prince Albert. I could go one better." He shrugged like it was no big deal. "Or maybe a magic cross."

I had a feeling it would be a big deal if he did it. Having three guys around with pierced cocks would be interesting. I wouldn't pressure the other three into getting them, but I wondered if they would consider it.

That was a conversation for another day.

"If that's what you decided to do, we would all support you," I said. "Maybe I should get a nipple piercing. Or one in my clit." Or rather, the hood. From what I'd read in magazines and online, that was the most popular piercing for women to get down there.

"I've heard those can make you feel really good," he said. "You'd look adorable with either of those. Or both. You know we would support you too if you decided to do any of that." He nodded firmly and his eyes shone with so much warmth my heart did a backflip.

I could easily fall in love with him too.

"That's sweet," I said with a smile. "I'll have to think about it." I may need a few more drinks of vodka before I was brave enough to have a piercing needle anywhere near my clit.

"You'd look adorable without them too." He lowered his mouth to mine in a kiss that started off soft and gentle but quickly became heated enough that I thought he would devour me. And vice versa.

We hadn't kissed until now, but it felt like our mouths were made for each other. Perfect size, shape and intensity. Even our tongues enjoyed dancing with each other. Sliding across our lips and brushing against teeth. He tasted like beer and steak. Delicious.

We finally came up for air before we forgot where we were. I doubted Alan would appreciate it if we started fucking on the dance floor. This wasn't that type of establishment.

Once I caught my breath, I asked, "Does Channing mind you doing that?"

"Not at all," Landon said lightly. "As long as we're completely open with each other and, usually in front of each other, we're both cool with it. It's like any good relationship. Communication is key. Like Zeke and Asher, we both want to be with you and with each other. As long as everyone knows what's what, I think we'll be okay. Don't you?"

"Yeah, I do," I agreed. "You guys are all something else. Most guys I know aren't big on sharing, much less like this."

"I don't really see it like sharing," Landon said slowly. "It's more like...we all want to be with each other one way or another. Like one big happy, crazy family. Y'know?"

"I do know," I agreed. "It's definitely crazy at times." I smiled. Happy? I could hope we would end up that way. Even now, there was so much hanging over our heads. The twins, Dante Fiorelli, the tour. After the tour.

It was enough to make my head spin.

"It'll be okay," he said as though he was reading my mind. "Whatever happens, we have each other's backs. Even if we decide to pursue solo careers, we will always be there for each other." He grinned. "You're not getting rid of any of us that easily."

"That's good, because I don't want to get rid of any of you," I said. I wasn't even sure I wanted this night to end. Tomorrow, we'd be back in the spotlight, for better or worse. For now though, I was going to enjoy being ordinary Abbie spending time with her extraordinary guys.

## 23

ABBIE

"THEY'RE GOING OFF TONIGHT." I grooved along with Blazing Violet. By the sound of it, the Edinburgh audience couldn't get enough of them.

"The band or the crowd?" Zeke asked. He stood beside me with an arm around my waist and his other over Asher's shoulders. He seemed more relaxed since the night in Wales. As relaxed as he ever got that was. He still watched for trouble wherever we went. That was ingrained at this point. And contagious, since the rest of us were vigilant as well.

"Both." I leaned against him, but didn't stop grooving. "I love this place. Not to mention the accents." It was hard to resist a Scottish accent.

"Oh, really?" Zeke turned to me and raised his

eyebrows. "Do we have to worry about you running off with some Scottish band?"

I pretended to think about that for a moment. "Maybe. There are some pretty hot Scottish bands out there."

"If they try to steal you away, we will end them," Tully said lightly.

"And dispose of the evidence," Asher added.

"And make it painful," Penn said.

"And messy," Landon said.

"Very messy," Channing said.

"I don't know if I should be horrified or turned on right now," I remarked.

"Both?" Zeke suggested.

"Definitely both," Asher agreed. "There's nothing we wouldn't do for you."

"Nothing," Tully agreed.

"There's nothing I wouldn't do for you either." We'd certainly gone through some crazy shit already. I hated to think what else we might have to do just to survive.

"Will you go out on stage and perform naked?" Penn asked.

"No," I replied. "I guess there's almost nothing I wouldn't do." After a moment I added, "Would you go out there naked?"

"I would if Zeke and Jackson would let me," Penn said.

"That's an easy claim to make since there's no way either of us would agree to that," Zeke pointed out.

Penn shrugged. "Not my fault if you two are too uptight."

"The world would never recover from seeing your cock," Asher said.

"That's a fact," Penn said. "Half the planet would want me and the other half would be jealous of me."

"Exactly," Asher agreed. "You don't need that added pressure on you."

Penn eyed him doubtfully. "I feel like you're being sarcastic but I'm not sure."

"Maybe I'm just being nice to you for a change," Asher suggested.

Penn grunted. He was obviously not convinced.

The crowd roared, signalling the end of Blazing Violet's set.

"You're up, gorgeous," Zeke said. He slipped his hand down to squeeze my ass.

Violet and the guys hurried down the steps, sweaty but grinning.

"Edinburgh is fucking awesome," Violet declared. "Best crowd yet."

After Penn helped me out in Wembley, I hadn't had even a hint of stage fright. It was almost like that night never happened.

Until I walked out on the stage in Edinburgh.

After hearing the crowd yell and scream, I expected, or at least hoped, to be greeted with enthusiasm. Instead, I got what sounded like a handful of clapping from the sixty thousand strong crowd.

I glanced back over my shoulder and gave the guys an uncertain look. They all gave me two thumbs up each. Then they were out of my sight.

I gave the audience a wave as I walked over to the stand and pulled out the microphone.

"Good evening, Edinburgh," I said into the mic.

The handful of cheers I got in response was underwhelming to say the least.

"How was Blazing Violet? Pretty fucking epic, right? They always know how to burn the place down." That comment usually got a laugh or two, but not tonight.

The crowd turned and started to chat amongst themselves. Those with seats sat down in them. Ouch.

Okay, it wasn't the first time that happened. I could deal with it.

I turned to Jewel and Macquarie as they settled in with their instruments. Macquarie gave me a shrug and rolled her shoulders.

Right, I would get no help from them. It wasn't their job to save me from falling flat. Nor could Penn come and save my ass again.

*This time, Abbie,* I told myself, *you'll have to save yourself.*

I nodded to the girls and gave them a subtle gesture by holding up three fingers. Change of plan. Instead of starting with the first song in the set list, we were going to start with the third. It was one I usually sang to the crowd after I got them going, but I needed to start with the big guns first.

That included talking to the audience like I knew they really came out to see me tonight, not the guys. It was all about me and the crowd. If I wasn't confident, I wouldn't win them over. I wasn't leaving the stage until I did.

"Did Blazing Violet wear you out?" I asked. "If you're that tired, I better tell Wolf Venom to go home."

That got the attention of some of the audience. They responded with some shouts and cheers.

"No?" I asked. "You still want to see them?"

They roared a little louder and some turned back to look at me.

"I don't know," I said. "They're backstage listening, and I don't think they're convinced. You're gonna have to be louder than that. Work with me here."

I lowered the microphone and walked from one side of the stage to the other.

I raised the mic back to my lips. "Let's try this again. Good evening, Edinburgh. How the fuck are you tonight? You don't mind me swearing, do you?"

The crowd got a little louder.

"You don't mind? That's fucking great. Did you come here tonight to have a good time or what? Excellent. Let's have a song or two and convince Wolf Venom that you guys are still awake."

*Here goes nothing.*

I nodded to the girls and started to sing.

I managed to sound like I wasn't even slightly rattled by their initial lack of interest. Go me.

Just as I hoped, the crowd started to get into the song. Bit by bit at first, then the rest of the stadium. By the end of the song, most of the place was back on their feet, dancing and clapping.

*You've still got it*, I told myself.

I gestured to the girls to go back to the top of the

set list. We would stick to the same order for the rest of the set, but the change did what I hoped it would.

"Some of you might have heard this song," I said. "It's called 'Inside Out'. I think most of us can relate to feeling like that once in a while."

The crowd roared in response.

For a new song, most of the audience seemed to know the words. A few of the people at the very front started to do the dance from the video making app, which made me grin. Thankfully, they were all dressed, so no one would bruise their own thighs with their cock. I'd hate to be held responsible for someone doing themselves damage. Especially to delicate organs.

"My name is Abbie Hart. Thank you for hanging out with me tonight, Edinburgh. You rock harder than any crowd I've seen on this tour." They shouted their appreciation and actually sounded disappointed I was finished. That was good for a girl's ego.

"Be extra loud for Wolf Venom!" I said before I put the microphone back in the stand. When I left the stage, the audience was screaming and cheering deafeningly loud. Perfect.

Smiling, I trotted down the steps and ducked into the backstage area.

"That was fucking epic." Asher caught me up in a huge hug.

"We knew you would win them over," Landon said.

"Not a moment of doubt in our minds." Zeke grinned and hugged me and Asher.

"I had doubts," Penn said. "But you proved me wrong." He waited until the others stepped away and surprised me by giving me a hug and a quick kiss.

I could be pissed off at Penn for his lack of faith in me, but that was just him. At least I knew he would always be honest with me.

"Did you just admit to being wrong?" Asher teased.

Penn shrugged. "It happens once in a while. Come on, let's get the fuck out there."

"Yeah, hurry up," I waved them all away. "I didn't warm them up for you for nothing."

They all grinned and trotted up the steps to the stage.

"You did good." Jackson stepped over to me and placed a hand on my shoulder. "An indifferent audience is everyone's worst nightmare."

I shrugged and tried to pretend I wasn't a little bit freaked out at first. "Nothing I couldn't deal with. In comparison to all the other things we've handled lately, this wasn't even top ten on my shit list."

"You're not a good liar," Jackson said warmly. "It has to be at least top three."

"It really is," I admitted. "But this is the job that chose us, so all we can do is roll with it."

"And that is why you're still around, while others have stopped performing," he said. "If you can't take the heat, stay off the stage."

"I don't think that's the saying," I pointed out. "But I'll take it. I have to admit, I wondered about the wisdom of sticking around in the industry after everything that happened with Vance and Pete. I wasn't sure if it was worth it. I could have gotten a job working in a supermarket. Go back to school and become a music teacher."

"The world needs more good music teachers," he agreed. "But you would have been wasted on the checkout, scanning people's groceries and lube."

I snorted a laugh. "Yeah, maybe." I'd probably want to give them advice on the right lube for them. And get fired after the first day. "It's something to think about anyway. Now things are back on track, I might stick around for a bit longer."

"You absolutely should," he said. "Levi is already talking about trying to move up the release date for your album. 'Inside Out' is going so well, we want to keep up the momentum. Don't be surprised if you get a couple of days back home before you're head-lining your own tour."

"No pressure," I groaned. I was exhausted just thinking about it. But elated at the same time.

He chuckled. "None at all. That's what you get for being talented and popular."

I couldn't complain about getting exactly what I wanted, could I now? I also couldn't help having a moment of self-doubt. It happened to the best of us. Yes, including Penn.

"Do you think people will come? To my concerts I mean." And the other way as well. I didn't mind being told my music was the sound-track to people's fucking. If I could get them to feel things just by singing, then I was doing my job and winning at it.

"They better," Jackson growled. "Levi is banking on it. He wouldn't back you if he didn't think your concerts would all be sellouts. Or close to it anyway."

Even the biggest names didn't sell out every time. As long as each venue was as close to capacity as possible, Levi would make his money back. And then some.

I smiled. "Abbie is back, baby."

Jackson patted my shoulder. "She sure is. And better than ever."

That might be a bit of a stretch, but I'd take it. I felt better than I had in a long time. Years. Like finally everything I'd worked towards was starting to happen. Really happen.

I turned my attention to the stage where my guys, *my band,* were playing better than I ever heard them. At the same time, a song started to form in my mind. That was happening more and more often these days.

Every single one of those gorgeous guys was my muse.

## 24

### ABBIE

"I LOVE DUBLIN," I said as I stepped down off the tour bus. "All of Ireland actually." Most of which I'd seen through the window of the bus, unfortunately. I added it to my list of places to come back to some day.

"In Dublin's fair city, where none of the girls are as pretty as Abbie," Asher said. He stepped off the bus right behind me. He took my hand and tucked me against his hip.

"You're going to make me blush," I said with a smile.

I felt light and relaxed after Edinburgh. Like maybe I could take on the world and win.

In the back of my mind, I reminded myself we had the rest of Europe and then America left on the tour. America in particular could be a very tough crowd. They tended to pay closer attention to celebrities' personal lives than some other parts of the world.

Some of the fans of Wolf Venom would take exception to me being in a relationship with any of them, much less all of them. Adoring fans were universal, and tended to get attached to their favourites. They would have photos of the guys on their phones and some may refer to them as their future husband, or whatever fantasy it was they had. Some would go as far as to hate me because I had what they didn't.

Obviously, there was nothing I could do about that. People thought whatever they wanted to think. I had no control over it and I wouldn't lose any sleep over it either. I'd just have to work harder to win them over before and during each concert.

No pressure.

"None of the girls are as pretty as me either," Penn said as he stepped down beside us.

Asher snorted a laugh.

"Of course they're not," I told Penn. "No woman is as pretty as you guys." I patted his cheek.

He grabbed my wrist and turned his face to kiss my palm. "Except you."

"And that was the exact moment we knew Penny melted like the rest of us," Asher said.

Penn shrugged. "You clowns wouldn't have stood a chance if I moved in first. Abbie wouldn't have looked at any of you."

"That's a load of crap," Zeke said cheerfully. "But if it makes you feel better to think that, go right ahead."

"Don't make me use my ninja skills on you three," Tully warned.

"All of you settle down," Jackson said. "You might not have noticed the press pack headed our way."

I stifled a groan. "Hopefully they'll play nice." They had in Edinburgh. We had a couple of interviews, but they were mostly interested in the guys. That was fine with me. At the end of the day, this was their tour, I was just along for the ride.

"What the—" Zeke frowned. "Is that the police?"

He was right. Two police officers were pushing their way through the press and telling them to stay back.

My heart started to race like crazy and my palms were suddenly sweaty. I tried not to glance at any of the guys. Whatever was going on, this could be about a number of things. Pete's death, Callista,

Vance, Poppy. Penn's run in with the evil twins, even something to do with Dante Fiorelli.

Or maybe the tour bus driver went too fast at some point and they were here to give him a ticket. I could hope, right?

"Good morning," one of the officers said pleasantly. Well, pleasantly in spite of the fact they were clearly there for a reason.

"Morning," Jackson said in the same tone of voice. "Can we help you with something?" He'd managed to move so he stood between us and the officers.

"We won't keep you too long," the other officer said. "We need to speak to Mr Cole."

All of us turned to look at Tully. His face was expressionless. With his training, he wasn't given to panicking, especially when there wasn't anything to panic about yet.

He stepped forward. "I'm Tully Cole. I'm happy to help in any way I can."

The first officer nodded. "Good. You'll need to come with us. The police in Perth, Australia want us to ask you some questions about the death of your adopted father, Xavier Lang." He waved towards a police car parked by the side of the road.

*Fuck.*

"Tully." I put a hand on his arm.

He patted it lightly. "It's okay. I'll answer their questions and sort everything out." But when he looked at me I saw real worry in his eyes.

The officers led Tully to the car and got him settled in the back seat.

I could hardly breathe as the car pulled away, taking Tully with it.

THANK YOU FOR READING! The story continues in Rhythm

# ABOUT THE AUTHOR

Maggie Alabaster writes reverse harem and, paranormal, sci-fi and fantasy romance.

She lives in NSW, Australia with one spouse, two daughters, one dog, and countless birds.

Jo Bradley is her alternate personality. She writes contemporary romance.

Sign up for my newsletter! Sign Up!

Join my reader group! Join here!

Follow me on Bookbub! Click here to follow me!

Check out my website- www.maggiealabaster.com

Book 1 Summoned by Fire

Book 2 Summoned by Fate

Book 3 Summoned by Desire


Shifter's Vault

Book 1 Discarded

Book 2 Deceived

Book 3 Disgraced


My Alien Mates

Book 1 Star Warriors

Book 2 Star Defenders

Book 3 Star Protectors


Academy of Modern Magic

Book 1 Digital Magic

Book 2 Virtual Magic

Book 3 Logical Magic

Complete Collection


Summer's Harem

Book 1: Shimmer

Book 2: Glimmer

Book 3: Flicker

Complete collection

Short reads

Taken by the Snowmen

Jingle All the Way

Also by Maggie Alabaster and Erin Yoshikawa

Caught by the Tide

Book 1–Pursued by Shadows

Book 2 Pursued by Darkness

Book 3 Pursued by Monsters

www.ingramcontent.com/pod-product-compliance
Lightning Source LLC
Chambersburg PA
CBHW020357120726
47904CB00002B/606